SINS OF THE FATHERS

KINGS OF THE MOUNTAIN BOOK 2

By Morgan Brice

1

DAWSON

"I think Lily left out some information," Dawson King yelled as he ducked a flying paperback book thrown by an invisible attacker. His breath misted in the frigid air, a sure sign a spirit was nearby.

"Ya think?" Grady King, Dawson's "step-cousin" and partner, replied as the EMF meter shrilled, indicating the presence of a strong —and pissed off—ghost.

"Fuck," Dawson muttered as he tried to move from where he'd taken shelter behind the couch, only to narrowly miss being hit by a coffee mug. It hit the wall and shattered with a *crack*.

They had hoped to deal with the ghost of Jason Carter peacefully. Jason seemed to have other ideas.

"Jason Carter! We want to talk!" Dawson shouted.

Two magazines and the TV remote flew off the coffee table to land in the middle of the living room floor.

When Lily said the ghost made her feel "unwelcome," she didn't mention an all-out attack.

"It's about Everett!" Dawson yelled, hoping the spirit had enough sense of self to hear and understand.

The room became quiet, although it remained freezer-cold.

Dawson and Grady rose slowly from where they had dived for

cover. Dawson had a sawed-off shotgun he hoped he didn't have to use, while Grady carried a bag with salt, holy water, and other items to handle a restless ghost. Grady took out a Ouija board and planchette, setting them on the kitchen table.

"We know you cared about Everett. And we know you saw him get sick. Everett had a stroke. He's alive but weak. The doctors don't think he'll be able to come home."

A gust of wind sent a glass flying from where it had been on the table. The planchette skidded across the board to stop on "NO."

Dawson's heart went out to Jason, worried about his long-time partner without news of how he was doing and now afraid of being left alone.

"Lily sent us here to talk." Grady tag teamed. "She knew you'd be upset. She also knew how much you two loved each other."

Lily Franklin was the long-time Meals on Wheels volunteer who had delivered to Jason and Everett for many years. She'd become a good friend and was Everett's emergency contact once Jason passed away.

A door slammed. Grady's head snapped up, and he shot a questioning look at Dawson. Dawson reached out to take his hand, intertwining their fingers and holding their hands in the air.

"We're like you and Everett. We understand wanting to stay together." Dawson picked up the conversation.

The planchette trembled before beginning to move. "D-A-N-G-E-R-O-U-S," Dawson said as the pointer moved.

"Dangerous to admit what you and Jason were to each other?" Grady asked.

The planchette moved to "YES."

"It can be, but plenty of people are 'out' these days. Even married," Dawson answered.

A framed photo rocked back and forth on the mantle. Dawson saw that it showed two men in their thirties decades ago on a sunny day, grinning with arms slung over each other's shoulders.

"If Everett can't come home, do you think you could go to him?" Grady asked.

The planchette went wild, circling "YES" over and over.

"Is there something here that means a lot to you that you could 'travel' with if we took it to Everett?" Dawson looked around, wondering what objects among the collections of a shared lifetime might be special enough to anchor a ghost.

A crash sounded from the back of the house. They headed toward the noise and found the door to a bedroom open and a painting on the floor in a broken frame. As soon as Dawson entered, he was shoved by invisible hands sending him stumbling toward one side of an unmade king-size bed.

He nearly fell, and when he braced himself against the edge of the mattress, he saw a leather jewelry tray on the nightstand, and in it, two silver military rings.

"These?" Dawson felt a puff of cold air in response.

"What are they?' Grady stood in the doorway, respecting the privacy of the old man who had lived there.

"Army service rings. Vietnam, if I'm right." Dawson picked up the rings and looked at them in the light.

"Lily said they met when Everett was a nurse at the VA hospital, and Jason came home wounded from the war," Grady replied.

Dawson's gaze went to a photo of a younger version of the two men standing together in uniform. They were circumspect in their pose, but Dawson imagined that he could see a slight lean, a bit less space between them than usual, and broad grins.

That could have been Grady and me if we'd been born then. I'm glad they found each other and were happy.

"I'll make sure that Everett gets the rings," Dawson said to thin air. "Can you attach to your ring? That way you can be where Everett is and stay together."

Another puff of cold air confirmed that Jason understood.

Dawson put the rings in his pocket and followed Grady back to the kitchen. He glanced around the modest duplex as Grady packed up his ghost hunting gear. The house and furnishings showed their age, but they looked comfortable and well-worn as if the men who had lived here were happy and content.

"Next stop, Oak Acres," Dawson said as he and Grady piled into his car.

Dawson's bright red Mustang Boss 429—nicknamed "Sally"—had a wide black stripe over the hood. The powerful engine was designed for stock car racing and installed in a limited number of street-legal cars. He'd rebuilt Sally from a junked hulk he had found in a salvage yard before he went into the Army. Grady had kept him company during those evenings and weekends that it took to bring the old car back to life. The months it took to restore the Mustang, and the evenings spent with Grady while they worked, were some of Dawson's best memories.

———

THEY WERE BOTH QUIET AS HE DROVE. MAYBE KNOWING THEY HAD Jason with them dampened conversation.

They found Lily sitting next to Everett's bed in his new room at the nursing home. Dawson spotted a few personal photos and knick-knacks that Lily must have retrieved from the house before Jason's ghost drove her out.

Dawson tried to see the handsome young man from the photos in the man who lay in the hospital bed. Everett was in his seventies, and the strain of his illness showed on his face. He had been fit in his younger days and was shorter and more slightly built than Jason, who had clearly been the more athletic of the two. Now he seemed too thin, and the aftereffects of the stroke dragged down the corner of his mouth and made one side of his body sag.

"Did it work?" Lily looked up hopefully as they entered.

Dawson withdrew his hand from his pocket and revealed the rings. "I hope the staff will let him wear them. They're what Jason chose as an anchor."

Everett made a low groan of relief, and his eyes opened. He looked directly at a spot beside Dawson as if he could clearly see the spirit who had hitched a ride. "Jason, you found me," he murmured.

The room grew cold, but Jason's presence didn't seem to affect the

4

equipment. Dawson couldn't see Jason's ghost, but clearly Everett could, and Dawson tracked Jason's location by where Everett gazed with wonder and adoration.

Did Jason's ghost remain in the house with Everett all these years? I want that kind of love—that lasts a lifetime and longer.

Lily slipped the rings over Everett's gnarled fingers, one on each hand.

"Thought I wouldn't see you again," Everett wheezed. Talking seemed difficult, and the stroke made it hard for him to speak clearly. Now that Jason's ghost had arrived, Everett had eyes only for him.

Everett managed a flirty grin. "You always were a rascal." His voice was warm with affection. He looked to one side as if turning his head to receive a caress. "Thank you for not leaving me here alone. They wouldn't let me go home to you."

Dawson found himself swallowing hard, overcome by emotion. A glance at Grady told him that his partner was tearing up as well.

Lily patted Everett's hand. "I'll leave you two alone," she said with a smile. "You have some catching up to do. And I'll make sure the nurses know to let you wear both rings all the time."

"Thank you," Everett said, glancing from Lily to Dawson and Grady, "for bringing my Jason to me."

"Glad to help," Dawson replied, and Grady echoed the comment.

Lily stood. "I'll visit tomorrow. Now have fun with your boy."

They headed for the doorway, and when Dawson looked over his shoulder, Everett had such a tender, joyous look on his face that Dawson felt tears streak down his cheek.

Grady fell into step beside him and bumped his shoulder. "Goals, huh?"

Dawson nodded, not quite trusting his voice.

"Are you boys up for a cup of coffee?" Lily asked. "The cafeteria here actually makes good java—and pie."

They went through the line and found a quiet table to enjoy their drinks and dessert, then fetched refills for the coffee.

"What made you aware of Jason's ghost?" Grady asked.

Lily touched her perfect blonde-gray hair, a nervous gesture.

"When I went to the house after they took Everett to the hospital, I wanted to make sure the trash was taken out and that nothing was going to spoil in the refrigerator. We didn't know yet whether he'd be able to come back."

"Everett was happy in that house," she went on. "He and Jason bought the duplex fifty years ago, right after Jason came back from Vietnam. Of course, back then, they had to tell everyone that they were 'brothers.'"

Dawson couldn't help a glance in Grady's direction. "I take it that wasn't true?"

Lily chuckled. "No. Their real friends knew the truth. They were two fools in love, definitely *not* brothers. The duplex let them pretend, for the sake of the prudes out there, that they weren't actually living together, although there was an inside door that connected the two halves."

"When did you find out about the ghost?" Dawson was acutely aware of Grady's thigh next to his on the booth's bench. Under the table, Grady put his hand on Dawson's knee.

"Jason died three years ago. Heart attack," Lily confirmed. "Until then, they both seemed hale and hearty. I don't think Everett and Jason were ever apart for more than a couple of days. Everett ran the second-hand bookstore over in Bryson City, and Jason ran the art and craft supply store next door. They were real pillars of the community."

"Back to the house," Dawson said. "What happened?"

Lily cradled the mug as she talked.

"When I went into the house, I checked to ensure everything was locked up tight; nothing plugged in that might start a fire, that sort of thing. I walked around, making sure none of the windows were open, but I swear I wasn't snooping.

"The longer I stayed, the more I felt like someone was watching me. I didn't see anyone, just a feeling, you know? I did what I had promised Everett I'd do and hurried out. When I glanced up from the street, I thought I saw someone at the upstairs window, but when I looked again, they were gone," Lily added.

"Do you think it was Jason?" Grady asked.

"Jason died in the house. I had met Everett through Meals on Wheels, and we became good friends. After Jason's death, I brought him food, stayed with him in the evening, tried to get him through it as best I could." She shook her head. "Poor man was inconsolable."

"Did you see the ghost again?" Dawson prompted.

She nodded. "Everett asked me to go back to the house and pick up a few things for his room and put the houseplants on the deck or take them home with me."

"What happened?" Grady asked.

Lily paused for a moment before speaking. "Everything was normal at first. I thought maybe I had just imagined feeling watched. I brought garbage bags and started to go through the refrigerator and the freezer. While I was in the kitchen, I heard something fall in the living room, and when I went to look, a mug was on the floor. I thought that was strange, but I picked it up and took it to the kitchen."

"And then?" Dawson couldn't help getting caught up in the story.

"Things went crazy fast. Doors slammed, knickknacks fell off shelves, chairs tipped over. I finally just looked up and yelled, 'That's enough, Jason!'"

She smiled. "I'm a tough old bird. It takes a lot to scare me. And in life, I certainly wasn't scared of Jason. I explained what was going on to thin air—about Everett being in the hospital and the stroke and all. We didn't know yet that he would have to go to a nursing home, but I tried to let Jason know that was a possibility. He didn't take it well."

She shook her head, remembering. "The sense of despair became overwhelming. And then the ghost had a tantrum. Throwing cushions, breaking glass, lights flickering, the whole horror movie vibe."

"So you think Jason was worried about Everett?" Grady chanced.

Lily nodded. "That's what I believe. I don't know for certain, but it seems logical. Jason saw Everett collapse and be taken away, and then Everett didn't come back. It seemed like Jason couldn't control his grief and anger."

"Do you know what's going to happen to the house?" Dawson asked, feeling a kinship with Everett and Jason.

"Jason legally changed his name decades ago so that they could pass for brothers. I don't think he had any family—or if he did, they weren't close. Everett has a niece, and she's his Power of Attorney," Lily replied. "I imagine she'll get the house ready to sell at some point."

"Jason wants to be with Everett—which means here at the nursing home," Dawson said. "I don't think either of them will return to the house. They'll move on from here."

Lily sighed. "That's good because someone—Everett's niece, probably me as well, maybe others—are eventually going to need to pack up their belongings. It would be nice not to have Jason throwing crockery at us," she added with a wry chuckle.

———

DAWSON AND GRADY SAID GOODBYE TO LILY IN THE PARKING LOT. THEY were quiet for a while on the way home.

"Thoughts?" Dawson broke the silence.

Grady sighed. "Thinking about a lot of things. Glad that for once a ghost hunt had a happy ending. Happy that Jason and Everett are able to be together—their whole 'til death do they part' is schmoopy and wonderful. Hoping we can be like that." He reached out to take Dawson's right hand, leaving him the left to steer.

"Yeah. Pretty much what I was thinking too. They had to lie about their relationship for decades, but they didn't let that come between them." Dawson gave Grady's hand a squeeze. "Like you said—goals."

"Look at the bright side—at least neither of us has to change his name!" Grady teased.

Grady's father, Aaron, had been adopted by Michael King— Dawson's grandfather—after Aaron's parents were killed on a hunt gone wrong. Michael raised Aaron along with his own two sons, Ethan, Dawson's father, and Denny.

Grady and Dawson had grown up together like cousins, but

knowing they weren't related by blood. Both of them felt the attraction between them in their late teens. Dawson, fearing that Grady's feelings were just infatuation, enlisted and left for four years to give them both breathing room. Despite a series of hurt feelings and misunderstandings, they found their way back to each other, reforging their relationship long-distance in the final stretch of Dawson's overseas tour.

It had taken several months after Dawson's return for them to get back in sync, but after a few harrowing near misses, they no longer doubted the strength of their feelings—or the reality of their love.

"I keep thinking about Jason staying on as a ghost with Everett," Dawson said. "All the jokes about being an old married couple aside, that's so sweet."

"And Everett clearly knew Jason was there," Grady replied. "I don't know if Everett could see other ghosts, but he definitely saw Jason." He shook his head admiringly. "Maybe we should re-write our vows to take out the 'parting at death' section and just plan to haunt each other for eternity."

"Sounds like a totally King thing to do," Dawson agreed. He kept his voice light, but his heart sped up at Grady's casual joking about getting married. They had known each other all their lives, and now that they were back together, their love seemed stronger than ever.

How long do we wait? Haven't we already waited long enough? I'm ready—is he? I know I don't want anyone but Gray—I've never wanted anyone else. How do I know when the time is right to ask? he thought, using his nickname for his partner.

Then again, we're still settling into the new house. We're practically married except for the paperwork. Waiting a few more months won't hurt anything.

Grady's phone went off, and he pulled it out of his pocket, thumbing it to be on speaker. "Uncle Denny? What's up?"

"Come home as fast as you can. It's Knox. He's in the hospital. We're not sure what happened, but it looks like an overdose." Denny sounded worn. "Meet us there—Colt's with him now."

"We're on our way," Dawson replied as Grady ended the call.

"I don't understand," Grady said, ashen. "Knox seemed to be doing better. He's been sober for a while. Colt's been good for him."

"We don't know what happened," Dawson soothed, knowing how Grady worried about his errant older brother. "Let's get the details and go from there. Things aren't always what they seem."

Grady's mother abandoned her husband and two young sons because she didn't like life in rural North Carolina and disdained monster hunting. That left Aaron to raise the boys with the help of Ethan and Denny, who rallied to help.

They reached Cunanoon General Hospital, and Dawson pulled up to the main entrance. "Go find Knox. I'll park and meet you in there."

Grady shook his head. "No. Stay with me. You know how things get with Knox. I love my brother...but he's not always easy to deal with, and he's worse when he's like this."

Knox was two years older than Grady, and he channeled loss and trauma into rebellion. A permanent injury while on a hunt sidelined Knox from the King legacy, so he took over the hardware store that had belonged to his grandfather, barely keeping it afloat. He struggled with addiction, despite help from counselors and the family.

"I've got your back," Dawson assured him. They parked and headed into the hospital together. Grady called Colt, and Denny came down to meet them in the lobby.

"Ghost problem go okay?" Denny asked.

Dawson nodded. "Turned out to be pretty straightforward, for a change. What happened to Knox?"

Denny motioned for them to follow into an elevator. "We're not sure. I believe Colt that Knox was doing better lately. He finished that stint in rehab—which only Colt could have gotten him to do; Lord knows I tried—and stopped drinking. The store was doing better because he paid attention to running it. I credit Colt with helping there, too. Boy's been good for Knox."

Colt Summers, one of Dawson's close friends, did his best to be Knox's guardian angel. Dawson suspected that Colt had fallen for Knox at some point while Dawson was off being a soldier. Dawson cared about Knox and respected Colt's intentions, but he privately wondered if Knox's demons might be more than Colt could handle.

"Then why?" Grady's tone was a mixture of hurt and anger.

"Like I said, we don't know." Denny ran a hand over his neck. "I'm afraid we're going to need to wait for Knox to wake up—and he's been slow about doing that."

"Is he going to be okay?" Grady sounded like a little kid.

"I hope so," Denny replied, worry clear in his voice. "I really do."

They followed Denny to Knox's room, and Dawson heard the hitch in Grady's breath when he saw his brother lying in the hospital bed, hooked up to monitors and an IV.

Colt glanced up from where he sat beside Knox's bed, holding his hand. He looked haggard, with dark circles under his eyes. "Hey, guys. Glad you're here."

Dawson and Denny hung back as Grady approached the bed. "Has he been awake?" Grady asked.

Colt shook his head. "Not really. He's been in and out, but he's not completely 'here' even when he's awake for a few minutes."

Knox's battles with depression and addiction had taken them all on a wild coaster ride of hope and despair.

Some monsters are harder to fight than others, Dawson thought. Grady, Denny, Colt, and Dawson had rallied around Knox when he and his father had been at odds, and after Aaron's death, they had tried to keep him from spiraling.

Through it all—the lies and broken promises, partial recovery, and relapses—Grady had refused to give up on Knox with a patience that made Dawson marvel. He shared Grady's belief that Knox was a good man with something broken inside and hoped that Colt, love, and therapy could turn his life around.

But first, Knox had to wake up.

"Do you have any idea what happened?" Dawson asked. "Knox looks healthier than he has for a long time—not too thin and good color. You two have been happy. Why now?"

"I can't prove it." Colt stared worriedly at Knox. "But I think he was drugged. I think someone slipped him some bad shit." He looked down. "I know how things were...before. But Knox has been different. Therapy this time seemed to click. He's done so well. We've been better than ever."

Colt let out a deep sigh. "He didn't relapse. Everything about this feels wrong. I believe in him—and I'm not going to doubt him now." He lifted Knox's hand to kiss his knuckles, then folded it between both of his.

"We believe you," Denny said, "but if he didn't do it to himself, then we need to find out who caused this—and why."

"And then we make sure they never do it to anyone else again," Grady muttered in a tone that promised vengeance.

Dawson edged closer supportively. A knock came at the door, and Knox's doctor entered, a trim woman with short brown hair who looked the right age to be his mother.

Colt rose, still holding Knox's hand. "Dr. Fairchild, this is Knox's Uncle Denny, his brother Grady, and Grady's partner, Dawson."

Dr. Fairchild nodded. "Glad you're here. We're still running toxicology scans, but frankly, we don't know what substance is responsible for Mr. King's condition. It doesn't match common street or prescription drugs. We thought at first it might have been a veterinary pharmaceutical, but those scans didn't match either."

"Did someone roofie him?" Dawson asked.

Dr. Fairchild shrugged. "When he was brought to the emergency room, we pumped his stomach—standard procedure. The contents were negative for the most common ingested drugs. We administered the standard overdose treatment, but he didn't wake up—which is very unusual. And the injection site we identified isn't where someone would normally inject themselves."

She sighed. "I'm aware of Mr. King's history. That's led to vein damage in the most likely sites. But what we found—frankly, the angle's all wrong to be self-inflicted. We reported it to the sheriff as a possible assault. I'm not sure he thinks there's enough evidence yet to support that theory."

"No, he wouldn't," Dawson muttered. Since hunting monsters

required a fair amount of rule breaking, the Kings and the sheriff rarely saw eye to eye.

The King family had named Cunanoon Mountain in Transylvania County, North Carolina, before the Revolutionary War and staked out the land for a homestead and the village of Kingston. Then they got down to the business of hunting monsters, which had been their charge from the British king back in their native Wales.

Few noticed that "Cunanoon" was the sound-alike for *Cwn Annwn,* Welsh for hellhound.

Their neighbors brewed moonshine, and while the Kings didn't run stills of their own, they kept the werewolves away from the bootleggers. Most young men in the Carolina mountains honed their driving skills outrunning the revenuers during Prohibition. The King boys out-drove vampires.

Dr. Fairchild ignored his remark. "We're running more scans. The substance has to match something. It's just very strange."

"Why hasn't he woken up?" Denny asked.

Dawson wondered whether Colt had asked the same questions and been turned away if he didn't have Power of Attorney. *Yet another reason not to put off getting married to Gray. I'd hate to be in a situation where one of us is hurt, and the other can't make decisions.*

Today might not be a good time to raise the issue since Grady was clearly upset. *But soon. It's tempting fate to put it off too long.*

"The large drug dose put a strain on Mr. King's system, and while the counteragents we use save lives, they aren't always gentle. Purging the drug goes rough on a person. We're letting him sleep it off. Since we don't yet know what he was dosed with, we're limited in what kinds of recovery medications we dare use. Setting up a drug reaction is the last thing he needs," she said.

I don't think she's telling us just how bad it was—or how close we came to losing him. Shit. I'm glad it doesn't look like an overdose, but that raises a big question. If Knox didn't do this, who did—and why?

"Do you have any idea when he'll come around?" Grady asked.

Dr. Fairchild gave a sad smile. "I'm sorry—I wish I could answer that, but it's going to be up to Mr. King's body to decide when he's ready. We're monitoring him to make sure he doesn't have any unexpected side effects, but he'll wake up when it's time. I wouldn't advise trying to hurry that."

After she left, Grady squeezed Dawson's hand and then let go, approaching his brother on the opposite side of the bed from where Colt had returned to his seat. Grady put a hand on Knox's shoulder. "Just be okay, Knox," he said quietly, tearing up. "We know this wasn't your fault. You don't have to hide. So come back when you're ready. I need you; Colt needs you—we all do."

He stepped back, stifling a sob, and reached for Dawson, who wrapped an arm around him. "Knox is tough. He'll fight this. He just needs more time."

Grady nodded. "I know. Doesn't make it any easier."

Denny turned to Colt. "Can you tell us anything more? Where was he? Who found him?"

"I'll tell you what I know," Colt said, with a worried glance at Knox. Dawson recalled reading that unconscious people could often hear what was said around them, and he wondered if Colt thought recounting the incident might further stress Knox.

"By the time I got the call, they already had Knox here at the Emergency Room," Colt said. "Denny and I are his emergency contacts, but they called me first. I read the preliminary report. Someone reported a man passed out in the alley behind the hardware store to the cops. Thought it might be a vagrant. When they found him, Knox was agitated but out of it. He couldn't respond to questions, and he tried to fight off anyone who got near. Then apparently he collapsed and was completely unresponsive. He's been this way since then."

Colt looked up at them. "But the thing is—Knox wasn't supposed to be at the store longer than to make sure paychecks went through. The process is automated, but he likes to check, just in case. He was off today. We were supposed to run errands and go to the farmer's market."

Dawson frowned. "But it was payday. Anyone who had been

watching for a while would have picked up on his habit of going in. So it was one time they could count on him being there."

Colt looked frightened. "You're right."

"To know that, someone had to be watching for at least a month —or know someone in the store," Grady said, sounding suspicious and angry.

"I'd like to think we can cross off the employees," Denny put in. "They've stuck with Knox through thick and thin. He's stressed them out—and has also done each of them some really good turns. I know anything's possible, but I would sure hate to find out they had anything to do with it. That's quite a betrayal."

"I don't think it was the hardware staff," Grady said, shaking his head. "The last thing they'd want is Knox in relapse. Things go much better when he's sober. He's a good manager when he has his wits about him. Hurting him hurts the store."

Dawson looked to Colt. "Has anyone from Knox's past been around lately?" He didn't wait for an answer. "Has he seemed nervous? Was he hiding something he didn't want you to worry about?"

"No." Colt sounded sure of his answer. "Learning not to keep secrets was a big part of his recovery therapy. There's nothing for him to be ashamed of, and I do my very best not to judge. We've put a lot of time and money into those counseling sessions."

He paused, then gritted his teeth as if having a silent internal conversation. "If someone from his past had come around, Knox would have told me. He's protective, and he wouldn't want them near me. He'd be an absolute tiger about it."

"Maybe someone turned up and took pains not to be noticed," Grady suggested. "But why? Knox doesn't owe money to anyone. We helped him clear those debts years ago. Even at his worst, he didn't use enough that stopping would put a dealer out of business."

"Maybe it doesn't have anything to do with Knox's past or his addiction," Dawson said slowly as an idea formed. "Not if someone hurt him to send a message to the Kings. Knox might not be hunting now, but he did for a long time. Long enough to piss off plenty of folks who were profiting by something we shut down."

Denny's expression darkened. "You're thinking this is more about the family than Knox?"

Dawson shrugged. "Maybe. We don't know enough for a good theory, but I agree with Colt that it doesn't sound like a relapse. And I know for a fact that the family has more than a few enemies. Maybe Knox was picked to send a message."

"Anyone who hurt that boy to 'send a message' deserves a special place in hell," Denny growled. "But if you're right, then we need to make sure someone's with Knox all the time—we can't give that person an opportunity to do more harm."

Dawson pulled Grady close and felt the tremors of anger and fear that ran through him. "We'll figure it out, Gray," Dawson said. "And then we'll take care of the mofos who did this to him."

2

GRADY

Denny offered to come back after dinner to give Colt a break to eat, shower, and get a few hours' sleep. Grady and Dawson promised to take turns sitting with Knox as well, and they worked out a schedule, all of them hoping that Knox would wake up and the vigil would end.

Dawson parked in front of the house they now shared, and Grady got out and grabbed his duffel bag, feeling like he was sleepwalking.

"Come on," Dawson coaxed. "Let's go in and get cleaned up. You'll feel better. I'll make coffee. It's been quite a day."

Usually, Grady found comfort in the familiar old house that had been the childhood home he shared with his father and Knox. Aaron had left the house to Grady, afraid Knox might lose it on one of his downturns. Aaron made provision for Knox, setting aside money equal to the value of the house in protected accounts. Even though Grady knew the inheritance was technically fair, he still sometimes felt guilty, although Knox hadn't seemed to care.

The century-old farmhouse had been purchased from someone in the large, extended King family. It sat on a couple of acres outside of Kingston, providing the privacy necessary for a family of hunters. Denny's house and the home Dawson grew up in weren't far away.

Grady had always taken comfort in having his kin nearby, even though he wasn't a King by blood since his father had been adopted.

In the months since he and Dawson had moved back into the old house, they had tried to keep the best of what Grady had grown up with while adding touches to make it their own. Sometimes though, like now, the too-familiar rooms brought back memories that threatened to overwhelm Grady with loss and remembered pain.

"Breathe." Dawson's quiet, patient voice broke Grady out of his thoughts. Dawson had come up beside him and rubbed a hand between his shoulders, soothing and calming.

"Some hunter I am," Grady said with a sigh. "I didn't even hear you."

"Your instincts are just fine. You didn't worry because your subconscious knew there wasn't any threat," Dawson reassured him.

Grady made a vague gesture toward the living room. "Most days, I see this as our house. But sometimes I see it the way it used to be, and it's a bit much, you know?"

A year ago, just before Dawson came home from the army, Grady's father Aaron was killed while on a werewolf hunt, and Grady had moved in with Denny. Grady still woke up shaking and crying out, struggling with survivor guilt.

If anyone understood, it was Dawson. They shared so much growing up together, even though for a while Dawson had been closer to Knox and Colt. That was back when the two-year age difference between him and Grady seemed like a big deal.

They had both lost loved ones. Six years ago, Ethan and Jackie, Dawson's parents—who were also hunters—died in a suspicious plane crash. Denny took Dawson in and did his best by him.

"There are a lot of good memories here," Dawson agreed, pulling Grady into his arms. "We played plenty of video games on the couch, shot target practice out back. But the best memories are the ones we're making right now—together."

Grady looked at the living room, focusing on the changes they had made. A new couch—wide enough for them both to lie down and snuggle—dominated the space, and a large braided rug in shades of rust and brown covered protective sigils carved into the aged pine plank floor. Photos of them together sat on the mantle and bookshelves, along with their combined collection of model cars and action figures from favorite movies.

"I love my brother," Grady said quietly from the safety of Dawson's arms. "But it's been hard sometimes. He's a good man with a big heart, but when Mom walked out on us, I think he always somehow blamed himself."

"You were both just kids. That was on her, not either of you—and not really on your dad either," Dawson replied, and Grady took comfort from the rumble of his boyfriend's voice and the beat of his heart.

"Knowing and feeling are different. And then hunting gave Knox a way to deal with all that anger. I thought he was always trying to prove himself—not that Mom was paying any attention. But after the accident, he couldn't hunt. I think he didn't know who he was if he wasn't a hunter, and he got lost trying to dull the pain," Grady said.

"He wouldn't be the first King or hunter to feel like that," Dawson agreed. "And I know helping him through the last few years wasn't easy. Uncle Denny kept me up on the basics even while I was gone. But you heard what Colt said—Knox was doing really well. We need to believe him and find out who did this."

Grady nodded. "It just seems overwhelming."

Dawson ruffled Grady's hair. "Then it's good you don't have to do it alone, isn't it? We'll figure it out. And whatever's behind it, we'll deal with it. Take things one step at a time."

Grady knew that Knox's overdose wasn't the only thing behind his mood shift. The one-year anniversary of his father's death was coming up, bringing all the lingering grief and guilt to the surface.

"Let's get a shower, and I'll heat up that leftover pasta from last night. Then we can crash on the couch and watch something that doesn't take a lot of brain power," Dawson suggested, and Grady loved him even more for knowing exactly the right thing to do.

Dawson guided him into the bathroom and got the water hot as Grady stripped and stepped under the spray. Dawson followed him a moment later. They hadn't had time to change after dealing with Jason's ghost, and the water sluiced away the sweat and tension.

"Turn around." Dawson squeezed shampoo into Grady's hair and massaged it into his scalp. Grady's shoulders relaxed, even as other parts of his body woke up from having a naked, wet Dawson pressed up behind him.

"Just let me take care of you," Dawson murmured with his lips against Grady's ear. Grady leaned back, giving his boyfriend access as Dawson carefully washed his body. A soap-slick tug to Grady's already-hard cock made him groan before Dawson set a rhythm focused more on releasing the stress of the day than romance.

"Come for me," Dawson urged in a husky voice that sent a shiver through Grady. "Let go."

Seconds later, Grady spilled over Dawson's fist, crying out with the force of his climax. His knees nearly buckled, but Dawson steadied him, angling his pliant body under the shower to wash away the evidence. Dawson held him up as he turned off the water, then helped him out and toweled him down.

"I'm not helpless," Grady protested without any heat.

"No, you're not. You're a badass," Dawson said, his tone fond. "But even badasses need TLC now and again."

"Not fair," Grady said. "I didn't get you off."

Dawson kissed him on the temple. "I'll take a raincheck. Right now, we'll both feel better if we eat."

Grady managed to get dressed without assistance, and once Dawson had pulled on sweats and a T-shirt, he headed for the kitchen. Grady dawdled, not quite ready to face conversation or his own thoughts. Soon enough, the smell of tomato sauce and garlic tempted him from his bathroom sanctuary.

"Sit. Eat," Dawson said when Grady joined him in the kitchen. Plates of steaming spaghetti awaited, along with tall glasses of water, and fresh-baked garlic bread. They sat and dug into the meal without conversation. Grady found that despite everything, he was ravenous. Judging from how quickly Dawson polished off his meal, it seemed like he felt the same.

"Go get comfy on the couch. I'll put stuff in the dishwasher and be right in." Dawson gave him a playful swat on the ass for emphasis.

Minutes later, Dawson joined Grady and handed him a bottle of beer. They sat close together as Dawson found a favorite action movie on streaming. They watched for a while, just enjoying the closeness and letting the beer take the hard edge off the day.

"I wonder if Jason and Everett ever thought about getting married," Grady said after a long pause. "They could have, even though they weren't young."

"Maybe they felt like they already were." Dawson shifted to make it more comfortable for Grady to rest against his shoulder. "Jason changed his last name to match, they lived together, and they probably had their wills and power of attorney set up for each other. Plus the rings."

"Yeah, but it's not the same," Grady protested. "I know not everyone wants to be married, and they say it's just a piece of paper, but...it means something."

Not that being married kept Mom from leaving us high and dry, Grady thought. *But it wasn't supposed to work like that.* He suspected that his childhood gave weight to the idea of official vows.

"You really want this?" Dawson's carefully neutral tone made Grady look up.

"You don't?" Grady felt a surge of insecurity and fought to tamp it down.

"Didn't say that," Dawson said. "I asked what you wanted."

Grady studied Dawson's face for a moment before answering and saw nothing but concern and affection.

"Yes," he said finally. "I know my parents didn't beat the odds, but I admired the way your folks got along. I wanted that kind of commitment," he admitted. "And after I got older, you starred in all those fantasies." He couldn't help the heat that crept into his cheeks at the confession.

"Oh yeah?" Dawson teased gently. "Good thing...because I thought about it a lot while I was gone. Intended to put a ring on it *and* a hickey. Let everyone know you're mine."

Dawson's words eased Grady's knee-jerk insecurity. They had grown so much in the past year, both before and after Dawson returned from overseas, learning to talk things out and not hide how they felt or put up a front. It was everything Grady had ever wanted with the man of his dreams.

Dawson turned so he could see Grady better, and Grady found himself holding his breath. *Is he going to propose?*

Denny's ringtone broke the moment, and with Knox in the hospital, not answering wasn't an option.

"Grady—nothing's changed, so don't worry. I just wanted to let you know that I got a call about a hunt that shouldn't wait—another restless spirits case that isn't likely to involve ghostly romance. I'm hoping you and Dawson can handle it. Colt and I will trade off sitting with Knox. If you're okay with that, I'll email you the details."

Grady met Dawson's eyes, questioning.

"Up to you," Dawson replied.

Grady suspected Denny had found the hunt to help take his mind off Knox. That didn't change the fact that people were in danger. They could put out the word for other hunters to handle the case— Cunanoon Mountain had plenty of Kings, most of whom were at least part-time hunters. But Grady also knew that sitting and watching Knox remain unconscious would be torture.

"Yeah, we can handle it," Grady said. "Send the info. We'll go out on it first thing tomorrow. With luck, we'll be done in time for one of us to take the night shift so you and Colt can get a proper night's rest. Or maybe Knox will snap out of it."

"We're all hoping that," Denny replied. "Thank you. And be careful—we don't need anyone else getting hurt."

———

MᴄHᴇɴʀʏ's Rᴏᴀᴅʜᴏᴜsᴇ ʟᴏᴏᴋᴇᴅ ʟɪᴋᴇ ᴛʜᴇ ᴋɪɴᴅ ᴏғ ᴘʟᴀᴄᴇ ᴛʜᴀᴛ would give even vampires and ghosts pause. The squat white cement block building sat back from the road, its single window crowded with neon beer logos. The name was painted in red on the wall, sparing the need for a sign. Even at noon, three Harleys and two pickups sat in the gravel lot. Grady doubted food was a big draw.

They had stayed up late researching the case Denny passed to them, trying to flesh out the information he had already compiled. Grady had been grateful for the distraction, even though he felt guilty for not keeping Knox as his sole focus. Dawson had done his best to absolve him, pointing out that there was nothing any of them could do until Knox woke up.

"Charming," Dawson muttered under his breath as they got out of Grady's truck at the roadhouse.

"They called Denny, so they must believe there's a real problem," Grady replied. "What the hell scares a bunch of bikers?"

"Guess we'll find out."

They were dressed to hunt in worn jeans, work boots, and flannel shirts over T-shirts under denim jackets. Both men had handguns holstered at the small of their backs, long knives sheathed on their belts, and Dawson carried a faded canvas duffel bag with suspicious bulges. Neither of them was looking for trouble, but only a fool would try to give them any.

The dim interior was lit by two television screens, more neon, and the rectangular fake-stained-glass light over the pool table in the back. Three men in biker vests sat at the bar, looking the part with long hair, travel patches, and tattoo sleeves. Two others sat at either end of the bar, clearly not with the bikers or each other. One man wore a blue repair company service uniform, and the other looked like a haggard salesman.

Everyone looked up when Dawson and Grady entered. Grady watched their expressions and could guess their thoughts. *First, they think we're too young to be here, then they realize we're armed to the teeth. Now they're worried that they're about to meet Jesus the hard way.*

"Can I help you, boys?" If the bartender shared the patrons' discomfort, he covered it well.

"Mickey called us." Dawson moved half a step ahead of Grady, speaking first because his lower voice and military bearing often stopped trouble before it started. Privately, Grady had to admit that both really turned his crank.

"Oh, yeah?" The bartender looked at them like he was trying to figure out a puzzle. "For what?"

"Heard you had some problems out back—after dark," Dawson replied, and a smirk hinted at the corners of his lips at the wave of uneasiness that shuddered through the regulars, making Grady wonder how many of them had seen things here they couldn't explain.

"What are you going to do about that?" the bartender asked.

"We're Kings. We fix problems." Dawson threw down the gauntlet, putting the next move in the bartender's corner.

"I'm Mickey. Glad you could make it. Hey, Red," he yelled toward the door to the kitchen. "Need you to cover for me."

A skinny young man with flaming red hair and bad acne came from the back, wiping his hands on his apron. "I've got it," he assured Mickey. "See if they can help."

Mickey's gaze swept over the regulars. "Don't none of you give Red a hard time, y'hear?" They all nodded, making Grady wonder what Mickey had done to earn their obedience, and what supernatural force scared the man who scared the bikers.

Mickey walked out from behind the bar and gestured for Dawson and Grady to follow him into the parking lot. "Thanks for coming. I thought the stories were just old wives' tales when I bought the place until I saw for myself."

Grady cleared his throat. "We know what you told Denny, but it would help to hear it from you."

Mickey looked uncomfortable, like recounting the tale was the absolute last thing he wanted to do, but he swallowed hard and nodded curtly. "Okay. Here goes nothing."

"McHenry's has been around since the sixties, kind of a fixture in these parts. Been added on to, painted different colors, had to replace the wall on the east corner after a truck ran through it. Had its share of brawls, a few of which are legendary," he added with a proud smile. "But no one wants to be parked in the back lot after last call."

24

His smile slipped, and his gaze flicked past the roadhouse. "It's not every night, but there's no telling when they'll be back. The regulars know the rules—and they believe. But now and then, we get someone who thinks he knows better. Sometimes, they get lucky and nothing happens. Sometimes, their luck runs out. Just last week, we found a guy screaming by his truck, all cut up."

"Do you know what did it?" Grady pressed.

Mickey rolled his lower lip between his teeth, and Grady knew the man was working up the courage to tell the truth. "Vampires. Least that's what everyone says."

Dawson raised an eyebrow. "Vampires? Were there puncture marks?"

"Look—I've seen the movies. I know how vampires are supposed to be," Mickey huffed, part bruised ego and part fear. "But I saw the security tape. Something appeared, messed the guy up real bad, and disappeared. Poof."

Grady and Dawson exchanged a look. "Did this 'vampire' move in a blur?"

Mickey shook his head. "No. Like I said—poof."

"Why would vampires pick your parking lot for their feeding grounds?" Grady asked, truly confused. *Maybe biker vampires?*

Mickey rubbed the back of his neck. His gaze kept flicking toward the back lot, even though it was bright daylight. "People say there was a house set back from the road on the same property as the roadhouse seventy or so years ago. A couple of locals turned up dead, and word went around that vampires did it—and that they lived in that set-back house."

The bartender hesitated, then visibly forced himself to go on. "A mob of townsfolk got it in their heads that they were going to get the vampires. So they went to the house and dragged the people out and cut their heads off. Then they strung up the bodies on a big tree as a warning. Couple of decades later, a guy near here admitted to killing the locals, said he made it look like vampires to distract the cops."

"The people you see on the security cameras that blink in and out —do they have heads?" Grady asked.

Mickey shook his head. "No. Damnedest thing."

"Is the house still there?" Dawson asked.

Mickey shrugged. "I haven't gone looking; folks say it burned a long time ago."

Well, so much for that *stopping the ghosts,* Grady thought.

"How do we find the old house?" Dawson looked at the woods with his hands on his hips, as if he could will a path to emerge.

Mickey pointed toward the back corner of the rear lot. "It's hard to see nowadays, but the old driveway originally cut through there to the road, before the bar was built. Look for the gap between the bigger trees—everything else has grown up with scrub. Might want to be back before dark."

They thanked him, and Mickey went back inside. Grady looked to Dawson. "Thoughts?"

"I think Denny was right that it's ghosts, not vampires. Want to bet that some of the victims have been descendants of the mob who killed the family?"

Grady nodded. "Yeah, I was thinking the same thing. Seems to go in cycles every ten years—probably on the anniversary of the deaths. That would track with the 'animal attack deaths' and missing persons reports we found in the records."

"So let's put an end to it." They stopped at the truck to pick up shovels, fairly certain they'd be necessary. Dawson hiked the duffel's strap higher on his shoulder, and they set off into the woods.

With the sun shining and everything in leaf, the walk would have been pleasant if it weren't for the potential fight awaiting them at their destination.

"I wonder why the mob thought the people in that house were the ones to blame," Grady said as they walked. In all their research, they hadn't found any kind of explanation, not even in the scant articles about the deaths.

"Could have been a grudge, or folks they didn't like living here, for whatever reason," Dawson replied. "All it takes sometimes is being 'odd.' And the kicker—the SPS and the HDF probably both claim the incident when they're trying to justify what they do."

"Ugh. Don't even mention them out loud." Grady spat on the ground for good measure.

"It's not bad enough that we've got monsters to hunt. We don't need that kind of trouble, but you know both groups would be all over this kind of thing," Dawson replied, kicking a stone in frustration.

Both the HDF—Human Defense Front, and the SPS—Supernatural Protection Society, were grassroots reactionary groups, and as far as Grady was concerned, domestic terrorists. The SPS avenged what it claimed to be crimes against people with paranormal abilities that eluded the jurisdiction of regular law enforcement. The HDF was their opposite, claiming to protect people without special abilities from cryptids and those with any form of magic.

"They're fucking vigilantes," Grady grumbled. *And everything we do falls right in the cross-hairs of both groups. We protect humans—and also the cryptids and people with abilities who aren't hurting anyone. And we do our damnedest to catch the folks that the regular laws can't touch.*

Here and there, Grady could make out signs that there had once been a dirt road, long overgrown, where they were walking. Slight banks on either side indicated the driveway's course, with trees on the right and left larger and older than those that had sprung up in the center.

They stayed within sight of each other, spreading out to cover more territory, still close enough to join a fight if needed.

Denny's research had given names and ages for the people who'd been murdered by the mob. John and Matilda Samuels, both in their forties. Isaiah Carpenter, in his early thirties, possibly a hired hand. The Samuels had bought the land and house from Hedda Thorpe, a widow who had built the place with her late husband between the World Wars.

"It wasn't fair to Hedda that people gossiped about her being odd," Grady said as they walked. "And it definitely didn't help that the place got a reputation for being haunted."

"Plenty of old women out in the country are folk witches and healers or have a touch of the Sight," Dawson responded. "They can defend themselves because they've got real ability. The people who get hurt are the ones who don't."

By the time Hedda sold the place, people already talked about the Thorpe farm having ghosts—and maybe a touch of darkness. Either the Samuels didn't know or didn't believe in that sort of thing. From the old articles Grady and Dawson found, the family got off on the wrong foot with the owner of the farm next door, who wanted Hedda to sell to him instead. The Samuels and their neighbor reported minor acts of vandalism they blamed on each other.

Then the neighbor's cow was found torn to pieces, and two teenagers went missing.

Frightened, suspicious neighbors needed an excuse and a target. Unfortunately for the Samuels family, they provided both.

"I can't believe that no one was ever convicted of killing the Samuels," Grady said, thinking that it was a beautiful day for such a gruesome task.

"You know what the small towns are like out here," Dawson reminded him. "That sort of thing happened more often in the past than we want to think about. Still does. Methods change. Murder doesn't."

At the end of the overgrown road lay a large clearing that was gradually being reclaimed by nature. A massive tree rose from the ground where the driveway ended. Grady could see the hints of what might have once been a flower garden, roses growing wild amid the weeds.

"The foundation's here." Dawson kicked lightly against a large stone set in the ground. They walked the house's footprint, but nothing of the building or its contents remained.

"You think there's a family cemetery?" Grady looked across the clearing.

"Maybe," Dawson replied. "But did anyone bother burying the ones who were murdered?"

"Shit. What if their killers just strung them up and left them for the crows?"

As soon as he said it, Grady felt certain that was what had happened. "Let's get the shovels."

Grady grabbed one for him and Dawson, who then took a forked willow branch out of the duffel. "Been a while since I dowsed for graves," Dawson admitted.

Tradition held that a dowsing stick in the hands of someone with talent could find hidden things—like fresh water, lost objects, and unmarked graves. Science might not validate the old practice, but plenty of granny witches swore by it, and the techniques were passed down by word of mouth from generation to generation.

"See, Daw? That psychic talent of yours is good for more than just giving you bad dreams," Grady teased.

"I keep telling myself that," Dawson replied. "Dowsing is better than visions." He didn't get visions often, but when he did they were usually premonitions of danger that left him feeling shaky and over-whelmed. While they had helped him avert disaster in the past, the dreams definitely took it out of Dawson's hide.

Grady carried the shovels, while Dawson had the willow rod. They stopped beneath the large oak, and Grady stared up into its branches, finding it all too easy to picture them laden with bodies.

"Here goes nothing," Dawson muttered as he took hold of the two sides of the 'Y' and held the branch straight out at waist height. He closed his eyes, and a look of concentration came over his face.

The end of the stick twitched, and Dawson walked slowly, looking like he was being tugged by an invisible leash. He circled the tree, and when he walked beneath a low, sturdy branch, the dowsing rod jerked in his hands, tipping sharply downward. Dawson raised an eyebrow, and Grady readied his shovel.

Dawson put the dowsing rod back into the duffel and took out a trowel, a shotgun with salt rounds, and an iron crowbar in case the ghosts decided to play rough.

Grady had a can of lighter fluid and a Zippo in his pocket, and he knew Dawson had a canister of salt in his jacket. He hoped they could send the ghosts on their way without a fight, but he doubted they'd get off that easy.

"Go slow," Dawson cautioned as they began to scrape away the layers of old leaves and fresh dirt from beneath the spreading branches high overhead. The tree's trunk was wide enough that Grady doubted he and Dawson could clasp hands around it with their outstretched arms.

They worked in silence for a while, slapping at insects and wiping sweat from their foreheads. Inch by inch, they worked their way down through the loam. Dawson's trowel hit something solid.

"Damn—tree root. False alarm," he grumbled.

Grady expected the same when his shovel met resistance. When a yellowed bone surfaced, he fought the urge to throw up. "I've got something."

He fell to his knees and grabbed the trowel, carefully clearing away the dirt that covered what looked like a human femur.

"I was really hoping the legends were wrong for once," Dawson said, sounding as nauseous as Grady felt.

Grady swallowed down bile. "If it's true that the killers decapitated the Samuels first, then they must have draped the bodies over the branches or tied the ropes under their arms to hang them in the tree. Like a backwoods gibbet."

"If they left them like that, then the bones are probably scattered all around here," Dawson said. "The ones animals didn't drag off, that is."

"And the people who did that got away with it." Grady's fist clenched at the injustice.

"They didn't go to jail," Dawson agreed. "But if the ghosts are still killing their descendants after all this time—there's rough justice there."

They worked a while longer, turning up more bones, which they carefully stacked at the base of the tree. Some were broken, others had been gnawed. Grady didn't need a course in anatomy to know that they hadn't found three full adult skeletons. Still, he figured they had most of the big bones for each of the victims, and finally, toward the bottom of the trench, they cleared around the tree were three skulls.

Grady murmured the words of an old blessing as he dug, hoping to pacify the spirits whose last, uneasy rest was being disturbed—and to fend off the dark, ancient entities said to be drawn to gallows trees.

"Do you hear that?" Dawson asked.

Grady raised his head. "Hear what?"

"Exactly."

When they hiked in, the woods were full of sounds—birds chirping, insects buzzing, and small animals scurrying through leaves. Now, an eerie silence descended over everything, and Grady felt the air turn chill. The hairs on his arms rose, and the trickle of sweat down his spine turned icy.

He set the shovel aside and grabbed the crowbar, as Dawson did the same and took up the shotgun.

"We're here to let you rest in peace," Dawson shouted to the empty clearing. "John and Matilda—and Isaiah. You've waited long enough and have taken your vengeance. It's time to move on."

Unseen hands shoved Grady and sent him sprawling, while an invisible force picked Dawson up and threw him to land—hard—several feet away. Grady hung on to the crowbar and came up with it poised to swing.

"Daw? You okay?"

"Watch out!" Dawson shouted as a gray form took shape right in front of Grady, the ghost of a man dressed in a plain shirt and overalls—with a neck that ended in a bloody stump. The lack of a head didn't keep it from zeroing in on Grady, reaching out to grab hold.

"Back off!" Grady swung his crowbar through the apparition, and it vanished, only to reappear a few feet away. This time, the ghost tossed him through the air like a rag doll. Grady let go of the crowbar to keep from injuring himself. He managed to avoid the foundation stones but knew he'd be bruised and limping the next day from the impact—if he survived, and his vision swam when his head thumped on the packed dirt.

A shotgun report echoed through the clearing as Dawson fired at Matilda's ghost when she loomed over him. But he'd spotted the threat to Grady and racked his gun for a second shot. "Get the fuck away from him," Dawson shouted.

The rock salt made the farmer's ghost vanish, and Grady ran for the tree, knowing their best bet lay in setting fire to the spirits' resting place.

An ice-cold, impossibly strong hand closed on Grady's collar and dragged him backward. He drew his knife as he turned and swung his machete right through the middle of a second man's spirit—which he guessed to be Isaiah's ghost—bisecting the figure an instant before it flickered out of sight.

Gasping for air, Grady dove for the tree as a shotgun blast roared over his head to clear the way.

"I'll hold them off. Light it up!" Dawson shouted, reloading. He used the salt to draw a ring around where he stood, a ghost-proof barrier that kept him from getting tossed about while he watched Grady's back.

Grady sloshed the dry grass, the bones, and the trunk of the hanging tree with lighter fluid. He hated destroying the old tree, but the ghosts were too connected to the place of their deaths for there to be another option. Dawson kept up a barrage of rock salt rounds, and Grady worked as fast as he could. When he had emptied the can, he flicked his lighter and tossed it onto the ground.

Flames roared up around the old tree, crackling on the dry bark and catching quickly in the scrub.

"Gray—get out of there!" Dawson shouted.

Grady turned to run, knowing that the whole field was likely to go up, not wanting to be caught in the flames.

All three ghosts blocked his path. Dawson's salt blew John's spirit to mist, but Isaiah grabbed Grady with rough hands, clearly intent on throwing him into the fire. Dawson wouldn't be able to get a clear shot with Grady so close to the spirit.

"Gray!"

Grady struggled, but Isaiah's rage-fueled spirit gripped him tightly enough to bruise, holding him off the ground by the upper arms so Grady couldn't swing his blade. His crowbar lay useless a few feet away where he had dropped it.

Fire engulfed the base of the tree and worked its way up the trunk, licking at the bark and catching in the small twigs.

Isaiah lifted Grady to hurl him into the blaze when they both staggered backward.

Small, strong hands ripped Grady from Isaiah's hold, shoving Grady away from the fire. He rolled and came up gripping his knife to see Matilda's ghost holding tight to Isaiah's spirit as she flung them both into the inferno.

John's spirit rematerialized as fire wreathed Matilda and Isaiah. An awful, ghostly howl of pain and fury echoed through the forest. Matilda held out her hand, beckoning for her husband to join them, keeping her other hand locked on Isaiah's arm. John's headless figure stumbled into the flames, and all three ghosts faded and vanished in the conflagration. Grady remained where he was, in shock over being alive.

"Are you okay?" Dawson shouted again, running to him. "We've got to get out of here before we get cut off by the fire."

Grady nodded, still a little out of it from hitting the ground so hard. Motion at the edge of his vision made him turn as a black shadow disappeared among the trees.

Another ghost? Or a spirit like the cu-sidhe *that are drawn to death places? I don't want to stick around to find out.*

Dawson pulled Grady along, forcing him to run to keep up as they ran back to the bar's parking lot.

"Are you hurt?" Dawson asked.

"Bruised. Got a headache. Could have been worse. You?"

"Same. Go ahead and get in the truck. I'll drive. I'm gonna stop and make sure Mickey calls the fire department before the whole clearing burns." He headed for McHenry's back door, then shared a short conversation with the bartender, who nodded and went back inside.

"I told Mickey that I thought we'd handled the situation, but to call me if anything else weird happens," Dawson recapped as he got in and started the engine. "Went to the back door because I figure the fewer people who saw us around here, the better," Dawson said as he drove away.

"Did you see anything except the ghosts?" Grady asked.

"Like what?"

Grady shrugged. "Probably nothing. I thought I saw a shadow-thing, but it could have been the firelight. It made me think of a *cu-sidhe*." Grady knew that the large, vicious faerie dogs were rare, but that legend fit what he thought he saw.

"If we hear back from Mickey that they're still having problems, we'll check it out," Dawson said. "Besides—any hellhounds in these parts are bound to the Kings. Dad told me that Adam King, the one who came here from Wales back in the day, made a deal with the faeries. We leave them alone, they leave us alone. The hellhounds and the protective elemental spirits in the mountains were the gifts from the fae to seal the deal."

"Adam must have had balls of steel to make a deal with the fae," Grady said. "But that explains why we don't run into them."

"Oh, they're out there," Dawson replied. "There are hollows in the deep woods where people never go. Those are *their* places. Smart folks don't bother them."

"It would be cool to have a pet hellhound," Grady mused.

"Uncle Denny has Angel. She counts."

Grady gave Dawson a look. "Yeah, she's a Rottweiler, but she loves butterflies and belly rubs."

"You've got to get past those teeth and that bark to get to the belly," Dawson countered. "She looks fierce enough to make someone piss themselves. The rest is our little secret."

They were quiet for a while as the miles sped past before Grady finally broke the silence. "Do you think the people who got killed by the ghosts knew what their ancestors did?"

Dawson seemed to think about the question for a moment, then shrugged. "Maybe some of them—but I doubt they realized that it caused what killed them. We like to think that the evil people do dies with them, but that saying about the sins of the fathers being visited onto the third and fourth generations? That's true far too often."

They came back to the house, and Grady ran a hot shower, peeling off his dirt and grass-stained clothing, eager to get the smell of smoke out of his hair and lighter fluid off his skin. He stepped under the hot water, and Dawson joined him a moment later, just as anxious to wash away the stench of death.

He didn't expect Dawson to angle them face to face, pulling Grady into a tight embrace. "Scared the shit out of me, Grady, when that damn ghost tossed you around. I was afraid you wouldn't get back up. And then when he tried to throw you into the fire—I think my heart stopped."

Grady hugged him back just as fiercely. In the heat of the fight, he hadn't had time to be afraid, but now that the danger was over and his mind replayed the scene in detail, Grady realized just how bad it might have been.

"I'm okay, Daw," he murmured, needing skin-on-skin contact to ground him in the living world and the here-and-now. "You kept shooting and covered me. That's what counted."

Grady's hands slid over Dawson's shoulders and arms, down his chest and back, quick triage from long practice, checking for injuries.

"I'm going to have some technicolor bruises from how I landed, but no blood," Dawson told him, doing the same careful assessment of Grady. They spoke in hushed tones like the shower was a confessional, a world apart from what lay outside the steam-filled room.

"Yeah, I'll be black-and-blue for sure, but no bones broken," Grady told him. "We're safe. We're alive. We're together. That's all that ever matters."

Pressed against each other under the warm water, there was no mistaking that both their cocks were hard. Grady pushed Dawson so that his back was to the shower wall, and they wrapped their hands around their stiff dicks, fast and dirty, as they kissed with a clack of teeth and devouring mouths. Sex as proof of life, not seduction, to take the edge off and reassure that they were both here and breathing.

Afterward, they soaped and shampooed quickly, in a hurry to let the fear and desperation wash away with the jizz, dirt, and ashes. A brisk towel off and fresh clothes left Grady feeling human again, although the hunt had fucked with his emotions, and he knew he'd see the hanging tree in his dreams.

"Come on," Dawson said. "Let's get some ibuprofen before we're moving like old men, and I'll order pizza. Don't feel much like cooking after all that."

Dawson headed for the kitchen to phone in the order. Grady wandered into the spare bedroom as a thought surged to the fore, and he felt the need to validate a memory. He went into the closet and took down a storage box he hadn't touched since he had cleaned up his father's things after the werewolf attack.

Which is how Dawson found him later, sitting cross-legged on the bedroom floor, engrossed in his father's hunting journal.

"You disappeared," Dawson joked. "Thought I might have to send out a search team." He paused, frowning as he spotted the book in Grady's hands. "What's that?"

Grady looked up and realized he'd zoned out for longer than he thought. "Sorry. Today reminded me of something Dad told me about a long time ago, and after we got out of the shower, I wanted to look it up and see what he wrote about it. I guess I got a little distracted."

Dawson sat down next to him on the floor. "The pizza still has another fifteen minutes before it'll be here. You can bring anything you want into the living room—easier on your back than sitting here."

"I really didn't expect to spend so much time," Grady replied. "There were some vampire hunts he did before we worked together, and I wondered how his lore squared up against our not-vamps today. Not as much in common as I thought, but then..."

"What?" Dawson's concerned tone suggested that he picked up on Grady's mood.

"I never looked through all of Dad's notes before. I kept my hunting diary on my computer and bugged him to let me transcribe his, but he always had a reason to put me off. If we needed anything from his old hunts, he looked it up. And then when he died, I couldn't bring myself to go through it because the memories hurt too much."

"I sense a 'but' coming..."

Grady nodded and looked up with wet eyes. "Dad's parents were killed in an explosion. Which is how he ended up being adopted by Grandpa Michael and becoming a King. But as time went on, he became convinced that their deaths were retaliation for one of their hunts. And, Daw, he believed that your father started to investigate, and that's what got your parents killed."

Grady met Dawson's gaze and saw the shock that mirrored his own. Grief, too, although Dawson's parents had been dead for seven years. Grady knew that mourning his father swelled and receded like the tide, better some days and worse on others, but never gone.

"Holy shit," Dawson finally said in a voice just above a whisper. "What if he was right?"

"If he was right," Grady said, surprised his voice sounded level when his feelings were a mess, "was there more to the werewolf hunt that killed Dad than we thought? Was he—were *we*—supposed to be next?"

"Knox got roofied," Dawson replied, and Grady could practically see the synapses firing behind his eyes as his mind linked information. "Random or related?"

"And what does Denny know?" Grady breathed. "Did his brothers keep him out of it—or did he hide what he knows to keep us safe?" He ran a hand through his hair. "Fuck—my brain hurts."

The doorbell made both of them jump. "Pizza," Dawson said with a weak smile, but Grady noticed that he slipped his gun into the back of his waistband when he went to open the door.

"Sometimes a pizza is just a pizza," Dawson said wryly as he set the box and his gun on the kitchen table. "Let's eat and leave the conspiracy theories for tomorrow."

Grady grabbed a couple of sodas from the fridge while Dawson got plates and napkins. They settled in to enjoy deep dish cheese and pepperoni. Grady hadn't realized how hungry he was until he smelled the food, and his stomach growled.

They'd made it halfway through dinner when Grady's phone sounded with Colt's ringtone.

"Is he awake?" Grady asked, feeling a surge of hope as he put the call on speaker.

Colt's pause turned Grady's hope to alarm in a single breath. "Colt?" Grady asked, fighting a lump in his throat.

"You'd better come to the hospital," Colt said in a somber tone that sent a chill down Grady's spine. "There was a problem with Knox's medication. Still not sure what happened—but someone fucked up and Knox..." Colt's voice broke. "He's fighting, but it's going to be close. Just—get here."

Dawson was already shoving the pizza box into the fridge and grabbing his keys before Grady ended the call.

"Come on," Dawson said. "I'll drive."

3

DAWSON

DAWSON PUSHED THE SPEED LIMIT. HE MADE THE NORMALLY FIFTEEN-minute drive to the Kingston hospital in under ten. Grady hadn't said a word during the drive, tension clear in every line of his profile, gripping the armrest like a drowning man with a life preserver.

"Knox is tough. He's going to fight," Dawson said as he whipped the Mustang into a parking space.

"I should have stayed with him," Grady said, miserable with worry.

"Are you a pharmacist? A doctor? Would you have second-guessed and double-checked every nurse?" Dawson countered. "That's not your job. We expect them to get it right—and most of the time, they do. But sometimes, they don't. It happens more than you'd like to think—even to people who don't hunt monsters. Take this one moment at a time."

He walked beside Grady with a hand on the small of his back to ground him. Dawson had always hated the smells and sounds of hospitals, even before his parents' death. Hunting meant injuries, no matter how careful hunters tried to be. Thanks to the King legacy and the family's influence in Kingston, their hospital understood the reality of the supernatural and specialized in areas far outside the skills of most health facilities.

Colt and Denny were waiting outside the ICU. Dawson found himself holding his breath as Grady rushed up to them.

"How's Knox?"

"He's alive," Denny said, and Grady visibly relaxed, although Dawson knew they both understood that was only the beginning.

"They think a nurse read the chart wrong and gave him a medication that has a similar name but does something completely different," Colt added. "We made it very clear that we expect a full investigation—not that it helps Knox at the moment."

"They realized the problem when his blood pressure dropped too low and all the monitors alarmed," Denny picked up the story. "Then there was a swarm of doctors and nurses, Colt got pushed out of the room, and they whisked Knox away."

"Someone gave him the wrong medicine, and I sat right there and didn't stop them," Colt said, guilt thick in his voice.

"Not your fault," Denny said, his tone softening as he spoke to the distraught young man. "There are supposed to be all kinds of systems in place to keep this from happening. Obviously, none of them worked—but that's not on you."

"He seemed to be doing better, right before," Colt went on as if he hadn't heard Denny. "His color was good, and his vitals were stronger. The doctor said they expected him to wake up later today. And now…"

Dawson clapped a hand on Colt's shoulder in support and got a watery smile in return. "Knox is a stubborn bastard. He likes a good fight. He'll get through this. Just wait and see."

"Tell me one thing," Grady begged. "Do you believe it was an accident?"

Denny glanced one way and then another. "I don't think we should be having this conversation in the hallway." He shared a knowing glance and motioned for them to follow him into the empty chapel, thoroughly checking to make sure they were alone.

"If we are working on the assumption that Knox was roofed for reasons other than sex, then someone had a reason to drug him. Maybe he knew something or saw something—even if Knox didn't realize the importance—and whoever did it wanted to make sure Knox couldn't tell anyone," Denny said.

"So him getting better put a wrinkle in the plan," Dawson guessed. "And they had a person on the inside try to finish the job."

"Do you know how insane that sounds?" Colt questioned. "Even for us."

"Insane is kinda how we roll," Denny muttered. "What else is new?"

"Do we know when the 'error' happened?" Dawson sensed that he had to be the objective one here since the others were too upset for analysis. He worried about Knox too—they had been friends all his life, close at one time, although less so in recent years. But compared to the others, Dawson realized he had the best shot at keeping some emotional distance and a clear head.

"I know when Knox got his most recent meds," Colt replied. "I didn't recognize the nurse, but then again, we've only been here for a couple of days, and I figured there were people who worked different rotations I hadn't seen before. That's the only reason I paid attention, but she didn't act strange. Nothing about the way she gave him the meds seemed unusual. I would have said something if it had."

Dawson could read Colt's self-inflicted judgment clearly in the man's expression. As much as he longed to lift his friend's guilt, he knew that right now Colt wouldn't be able to hear any consolation.

"Do we know who the nurse was?" Dawson pressed. "Is she a regular you just hadn't met, or someone filling in last-minute? A hospital employee or a temp?" An ugly suspicion had begun to form in his mind, and he hoped by all that was holy that he was wrong.

Colt shrugged, looking helpless and angry. "I asked all those questions. The hospital brass hasn't gotten back to me, and the treatment staff was too busy saving Knox."

"We'd better go back out to the hall—they need to find us when there's news," Grady pointed out.

"Look sharp," Denny muttered. Dawson and the others turned to see Dr. Fairchild coming toward them, looking harried.

Colt and Grady hurried to meet her, while Denny and Dawson hung back, close enough to hear but letting the others take the lead.

"How's Knox?" Grady practically vibrated with tension.

"Do you know what drug did this?" Colt followed up.

Dr. Fairchild held up a hand to stay their questions. "Knox is alive, and we don't believe he suffered any permanent damage, largely because we were able to intervene so quickly." She looked to Colt. "Which happened thanks to your quick thinking."

Colt looked down, and his cheeks colored. "Just watching out for him."

"Knox is back in the ICU, and he's unconscious, but as far as all our scans can tell, it's a normal reaction to the stress that the medication error put on his body," she continued. "So I'd like to ask you not to visit him tonight. Let him get a solid twelve hours of sleep. Rest really is the best medicine."

"Begging your pardon, but after what just happened, I think we should have one person in the room with Knox at all times," Denny said. "We'll let him sleep, and we won't get in the way of the staff, but until we know all the details about the medication 'error,' I'm going to have to insist."

Dawson could see understanding dawn on her face. "You think that someone did it on purpose?" she said, eyes wide.

"I think it's a possibility that needs to be ruled out," Denny replied. "You know what the Kings are known for—besides the auto body shops. We've made our share of enemies. There's just something off about this whole 'overdose' situation that makes my Spidey sense tingle."

Dr. Fairchild swallowed hard, then nodded. "Alright. That can be arranged. It's not normal protocol, but exceptions can be made. I'll take care of it."

"Thank you." Denny cleared his throat. "Has anyone talked to the nurse who administered the medicine? I assume the hospital would like to know how this could happen."

Dr. Fairchild looked uncomfortable. "We're looking into that. There seems to have been some confusion over the rotation assignments. The usual nurse wasn't on duty."

"I saw the nurse who gave the most recent meds," Colt volunteered. "I can describe her."

Fairchild led him to the nurses' station, and Colt gave the description to the duty nurse.

"We didn't have anyone matching that description on the roster last night," the nurse said, clearly concerned. "I'm calling security. They can check the video feeds."

Dawson and Grady waited for Knox to be transferred to a room while Denny and Colt went with the nurse. They came back half an hour later, looking out of sorts.

"Well, it just gets murkier," Denny grumbled. "No one recognizes the 'nurse' who gave Knox the wrong meds. But we did get one good frame of her face off one of the security videos, so I sent it to our whiz kid friends to see if they can dig up any intel."

Through the years, they had made friends with others in the supernatural hunting community beyond Cunanoon Mountain. Some of those allies were well-versed in the occult, while others were excellent hackers and data miners armed with both skills and magic.

"I still want to know why," Colt fumed. "Knox doesn't even hunt—hasn't for years. Why him...and why now?"

"Once he wakes up, we'll talk to him, maybe get some answers," Dawson replied. "Right now, we've got to make sure that happens." He sighed. "I'll call the auto body shop and the hardware store and let them know to have someone cover our shifts for the next couple of days. We don't need whatever this is bleeding over to the civilian businesses."

The other King legacy—besides monster hunting—was a chain of auto body shops across Transylvania County, started by their great-grandfather. That income supported their monster hunting activities, and nearly everyone had a role to play. Grady didn't have the mechanical aptitude that came so easily to Dawson. But while Dawson was great with the nuts and bolts side of cars, Grady was good with computers. That made learning the high-tech side of diagnostics and onboard systems easy.

Denny's phone rang with a tone Dawson knew meant hunter business. He swore under his breath and walked down the hall, talking in quiet tones until he ducked into an alcove for privacy. When he came back, he looked concerned and pissed off.

"We've got a situation. Two packless coyote shifters were found murdered near a barn where they'd been squatting. Looks like they might have Syndicate ties. You know Sheriff Rollins isn't going to like that one bit," Denny said.

He looked to Dawson. "Let's go down to the coroner's and see what we can find. Grady and Colt can hold the fort here."

"Once Knox is back in a room, Colt and I can ward it and lay down salt and sigils," Grady offered. "We've got this."

Dawson felt torn, but he knew Colt and Grady could handle keeping an eye on Knox—and defending him if it came to that. And given the long-time bad blood between Rollins and the King family, being Denny's wingman might keep his uncle out of jail.

"Okay, but call if you need anything," Dawson warned.

Grady nodded. "Will do. Try not to get arrested. Or Tasered."

Dawson rolled his eyes. "You make it sound like that happens all the time."

"More than it does to most people," Grady countered. "This family doesn't bring out the best in the sheriff."

Back in high school, Ethan and Aaron King had decided to teach Rollins and his shifter-jock friends a lesson for being assholes. The two King brothers had taken Rollins out drinking and gotten him black-out drunk.

When Rollins woke up, he was naked, lying on the cold steel of the veterinarian's operating room table, with his balls wrapped in gauze and a brochure on *"Care for your Neutered Pet"* lying on his chest.

Photos were rumored to exist. It took a panicked call to the vet to discover that no surgery had been done, and Rollins took a lot of ribbing afterward. Despite the decades that had passed, Rollins had never forgotten the incident or fully forgiven the King brothers. That extended to Denny, who hadn't been part of the prank.

"I'll make sure he behaves," Denny told Grady. "You boys keep a sharp eye out for anything hinky going on. I'll let you know what I hear from my research guys."

Dawson left the Mustang for Grady and climbed into Denny's truck. "I know you're thinking that this shifter thing is important, or we wouldn't be jumping on it so fast. What's up?"

"The Syndicate has been lying low for a while—and I can't say that I missed them," Denny said. "Ever since that warlock up near Boone disappeared, they've kept their heads down. Would've been nice if it had been permanent, but luck never works that way."

The Kings were the guardians of Cunanoon Mountain and their corner of Western North Carolina, hunting the worst of the worst. They tended to look the other way at cryptids and supernatural beings that didn't kill people or cause havoc. That included a fragile "truce" with the cluster of sentient creatures who ran a loose network of shady businesses. Some of those the Kings left to the human authorities, while others they ignored unless disappearances or bodies made it their business.

Vampires ran the betting parlors, bootlegging, and the strip joints showcasing sirens as an irresistible attraction. The last Dawson heard, an incubus and a succubus ran the local sex trade. Rumor had it the fae were bankers and attorneys for other paranormal creatures, along with dabbling in a bit of white-collar crime. Most of the time, those groups evaded human scrutiny by keeping a low profile.

Werewolves were the exception since they went for the rough work—loansharking, protection money, cargo theft, and chop shops. It helped that the Transylvania County Sheriff and most of his deputies were shifters—which meant they weren't dependent on the moon and possessed extra strength and speed.

For the most part, things stayed civil. Hunters knew that the supernatural factions also had witches, cryptids, and ghosts on their side and paid off human helpers to evade notice. Sometimes, they even reported rogues to the Kings because the danger was bad for business.

Whoever killed the coyote shifters and tossed the bodies where they were sure to be found was making a statement—and a threat.

But who's supposed to get the message—and what does it mean?

The police were gone by the time Dawson and Denny reached the scene. Dawson didn't doubt that the sheriff would follow procedures. Rollins was competent and, regardless of his tiffs with the Kings, generally did a good job of keeping the peace and stopping the bad guys.

But despite being a shifter himself, Rollins wasn't a hunter. He didn't have the training or experience that the Kings handed down from generation to generation or the background in occult lore. Which meant that even with forensics, the deputies might have missed something.

"Not enough blood," Denny observed as they carefully walked around the dark-stained spots in the tall grass. "Probably means they were killed somewhere else and dumped so they'd be noticed."

"If they weren't part of a local pack, why were they here?" Dawson mused.

The coyote shifters who settled on Cunanoon Mountain were a decent lot, despite old prejudices about their animal side. They didn't bother livestock or pets, stayed out of trouble, and went a little over-board in their enthusiasm to be community volunteers. Dawson hoped that if word got around about the murders, it wouldn't spark retaliation against the law-abiding packs.

"Stir up trouble?" Denny speculated as they both walked in ever-widening circles around where the bodies had been found, looking for anything the cops might have missed.

"Send a warning? Get revenge?" Dawson added.

"Muddy the waters? Get everyone upset, so we aren't paying atten-tion to the real issue? Something about this whole thing feels off," Denny muttered.

The cops had already been at the scene, so footprints and tire tracks had been compromised. Dawson hoped they might find something the police had overlooked, a connection to a supernatural killer. But after half an hour, he and Denny had to admit that either the sheriff's team had been exceptionally thorough, or the murderer had left nothing behind.

"Why would anyone want to flip off the Syndicate?" Dawson asked as they walked back to the truck. "It's poking the bear. Who benefits?"

Denny started the engine and turned the truck around for the drive back to town. "Could be an upstart player who wants attention. Or maybe some kind of internal rivalry that wasn't supposed to spill over where outsiders could see."

"Well, that was a total fail." Dawson drummed his fingers on the armrest. His mind flashed back to the conversation with Grady the night before, and he opened his mouth to ask a question, then closed it without saying anything. *Too much going on to dig up old secrets. Let's get Knox out of the hospital and take things one step at a time.*

"I'll get our hacker friends to see if they can turn up anything about missing shifters or break into the sheriff's system and see what the cops know." Denny pulled out his phone and sent a text. "There's a connection. We just have to find it."

Dawson couldn't help feeling restless and depressed on the way back to the hospital. Seeing the crime scene hadn't offered any insights, and he couldn't shake the sense that they were missing something that was right in front of them. Desperate to keep his thoughts from spinning, Dawson decided to change the subject.

"What do you think really happened to Knox?"

"You mean before or just now?"

Dawson shrugged. "Either. Both."

Denny didn't answer right away, but from the set of his jaw and his tight grip on the wheel, Dawson knew his uncle's mind was hashing out possibilities.

"I know Knox has had some dark times, but I think his turn-around was real. Colt's been good for him—they're sweet together, and I think their relationship gives Knox something of his own to fight for," Denny said after a pause.

"He's going to therapy and doing a weekly support group. Got sober and put all that extra energy into Colt and the hardware store. So I don't think it was a relapse—but someone *wants* us to think that," Denny went on. "As for the medication 'error,' I've got a bad feeling that we're going to find out it was an attempt on Knox's life."

Dawson nodded. "Yeah. That's what I think too. They were hoping that Knox would die of an 'overdose' and no one would question it," he added bitterly. "Except we saved him. So they tried again to make it look like an accident. That's a lot of effort. Whatever they think he knows, it's a bombshell."

Once again, he had a question on the tip of his tongue about whether Knox's situation could be connected to the deaths of Grady's grandparents and Dawson's parents. *Grady deserves to be in on that conversation. It can wait until both of us can hear what Denny has to say.*

When they got back to the hospital, Grady was taking his turn sitting with Knox while Colt sat in the waiting area with a sandwich and a cup of coffee.

"Find anything?" Colt asked as they joined him.

Dawson shook his head. "Nothing except that someone transported the bodies to that spot. How about you?"

Colt swallowed a bite of his ham and cheese and washed it down with a slug of coffee. "Grady and I got the room locked down as tight as we can with every protection they'd let us get away with in the hospital," he reported. "Checked the room for hexes and curse bags too."

"I've got some amulets back at the house all four of you should be wearing," Denny said. "I'll run back and get them. They were made by people who really know their stuff. Bought them for the holidays, but now seems like as good a time as any. So, Merry Christmas."

"And I've got a clue—maybe," Colt said. "They gave me Knox's wallet for safekeeping. I got to thinking that maybe something would give us an idea of where he'd gone the night he got roofied. I called his assistant manager at the store, who told me that Knox got a call at work when he stopped in to do paychecks and said he needed to deal with a problem. A customer had bought a vital piece of equipment from the store, and it wasn't working right."

"I could see Knox going to see for himself," Dawson replied. "Especially if it was a big item."

"So I looked in his wallet to see if he wrote down an address or took notes from the call. And I found this." He held out a receipt for a soft drink from The Maverick, dated two days ago.

"Wait—I've driven past this place. Dive bar. Might have been somewhere Knox used to go but wouldn't be on his list since he cleaned up his act," Dawson said.

"Yeah, I know where it is," Colt said with distaste. "Not even somewhere Knox hung out back in the bad old days—and I should know since I hauled Knox's sorry ass out of most of the bars in Transylvania County. I can't imagine that he'd go there unless it was the bar that had bought an expensive appliance that wasn't working. And the call came before usual 'bar hours,' so he might have expected it to be mostly empty—that crowd shows up a lot later."

"Does anyone know what the bar bought?"

"That's just it," Colt answered. "I called the bar and spoke to the owner. They did buy a dishwasher and a garbage disposal from the store—special order. And they did have a problem with the dishwasher. He says that Knox showed up for the service call and fixed it —it was a setting that had gotten messed up. Then the manager got called to the back to deal with an issue, and when he came back, Knox was gone."

"Shit. This stinks of a setup," Denny said. He looked to Colt. "When are you and Grady due to trade off?"

"Any time now," Colt replied. "I just wanted to get a bite to eat before I settle in for the night."

Denny glanced at Dawson. "Sounds like it might be worth a trip for you and Grady to visit The Maverick and see what you can turn up. Just keep your heads down—and stay sharp. I'm going home and working my contacts to see if we can find out more about the fake nurse and the dead shifters."

———

Dawson and Grady pulled up at The Maverick around eight o'clock that night, before the crowd got rowdy, but after the parking lot began to fill. He drove Denny's pickup because the Mustang definitely didn't fit in here; far too memorable for them to be incognito. He spotted a black Corvette parked in the shadows and raised an eyebrow, wondering who was slumming and if they knew what they were in for.

They intentionally "dressed down" for the evening, choosing jeans, T-shirts, and flannels barely a step above what they'd wear to go hunting, along with battered boots.

While they didn't want trouble, both men prepared for the worst, each carrying a small concealed arsenal, right down to shivs in their boots. *Looks like the kind of place where I want to take a gun to a knife fight.*

"A hazmat suit might be appropriate," Grady said as they eyed the bar.

"Don't bend over the pool table, and don't shine a UV light in the men's room," Dawson joked.

"Thanks for that. Now I have to bleach my brain."

Dawson didn't mind the danger—he and Grady could handle themselves against much worse than a rowdy bunch of bikers. It galled him to have to pass for straight to avoid trouble when he'd been out and proud since his early teens.

Dawson walked in first and took a seat at a table. He had his back to the wall and a clear view of the interior. Grady came in a few minutes later and pulled up a stool at the bar, flagging the bartender to order a drink.

"What're you having?" The server who came to wait on Dawson looked like she'd pulled a double shift.

"Coke and a burger with fries," he answered, not needing a menu and not planning to eat much of the food. He needed a reason to hang out, and dawdling over his meal would suffice.

Grady was doing what he did best, chatting up the bartender and trading comments about the game on the big screen over the bar. He'd probably nurse his beer for the full time they stayed, but even a second drink wouldn't challenge his tolerance.

Dawson looked toward the bar with the pretense of checking the score on TV, although he scanned the patrons instead. A working-class roadhouse in rural North Carolina didn't expect an upscale crowd. Deer antlers, prize buck photos, and bowling trophies decorated the walls and shelves. The only celebrity photos were of a third-rate pro wrestler who was from the area and a local politician now serving jail time for corruption.

When his burger came, Dawson shifted in his chair for a look at the rest of the customers seated at tables. He guessed that most were somewhere between late twenties and early forties, with a haggard look that easily added a decade to their real age.

A tall, dark-haired man standing at the end of the bar caught Dawson's attention. *He looks a little too well-groomed to be here. And he's trying to look casual, but he's wound tight. Wonder if he's the one with the 'Vette.*

He heard Grady laugh and wondered what he was talking about with the bearded redhead on the stool next to him. They seemed to have bonded over something, and Dawson knew Grady was pumping his companion for information.

The tall man's gaze flickered to Grady and his new "friend" before quickly looking away. The glance lasted seconds, but Dawson thought he read a range of reactions in the stranger's blue eyes. *Concern. Curiosity. And...possessiveness? Are they together and working the room separately like Gray and me? If so, whose side are they on—and why are they here?*

Dawson felt the tall stranger's gaze land on him like a spotlight. His expression shifted to annoyance, assessment, and possibly, recognition. Dawson played it cool, although his heartbeat quickened at the possibility that the man he didn't know recognized him.

Many of the customers wore denim jackets or biker vests with patches. As he nibbled his burger, Dawson idly read the patches. He saw a number of pyramids with red apex. Some patches read *HR4HO*, *D2C*, and **D33P6FR33KS*.

I've seen those before. Shit. Where did I see them?

In the next breath, Dawson remembered and froze.

Human Rights For Humans Only. Death to Cryptids. Deep-six Freaks. Fuck. This bar's a Human Defense Front hangout. We've got to get out of here before we end up like Knox.

Dawson did his best to school his face to give nothing away in his expression. He forced himself to eat a few more bites so his departure wouldn't look suspicious, all the while keeping an eye on Grady and trying to scan for threats.

He threw down enough bills to cover the food and a tip, skidding the chair across the sticky floor. Dawson saw Grady's shoulders flinch and knew his signal had been received.

He fought the urge to grab Grady and run, but he knew that their best chance of getting out lay in not attracting attention.

Dawson sauntered toward the door, only to have two large men block his path.

"You're one of them Kings, ain't you?" the burly man on his left said.

"Freak protectors, that's what you are," the bouncer-sized man to the right added. "Betraying humans. You shouldn't have come here."

Dawson felt Grady step up behind him. He knew they were both armed, but he didn't want to turn this into a bloodbath.

"Which of you drugged Knox?" Dawson challenged.

"The addict? Why d'ya think he needed any help?' the bouncer mocked. "Probably just needed a fix."

"You lured him here," Dawson accused. "And then you drugged him. Why?"

Out of the corner of his eye, Dawson saw the crowd gather, eager to see a brawl.

"Why don't you ask him? If his brains aren't too scrambled to remember," the burly man taunted. "Just proves he's as much of a freak as those monsters you people protect."

"Get out of our way," Dawson growled. *They want a fight? Let's get this party started.*

The bouncer swung, Dawson ducked and brought his boot up sharply into the big man's nuts, following up with an elbow to the neck as the man sagged to the ground.

The bystanders with HDF patches surged forward, and then Dawson and Grady were in the thick of things, fists flying.

A man launched himself at Grady from atop the bar, and Grady grabbed him by the arm, stepping aside and flipping him to land hard on the floor. Dawson saw the glint of a blade and dodged, letting the knife slide through his sleeve but miss cutting deeply into his arm. He pulled his own knife, leaving his attacker with a slice across the chest that would hurt like hell but not be life-threatening.

Grady's left hook flattened one man, but he took a punch in return that sent him staggering. Dawson kicked Grady's attacker in the side of the knee, hearing a satisfying snap as the man went down howling.

Two more bikers came at Dawson, while a guy big enough to be two people went after Grady. Dawson managed to dodge another knife thrust, twisting the attacker's arm until he felt the joint pop. It seemed their opponents were used to winning on size and strength without real training, a weakness Dawson knew he could use.

"Watch out!" Grady shouted as a guy the size of a refrigerator lunged at Dawson, swinging a nightstick.

Dawson threw himself to one side, missing the worst of the strike. He heard a loud crunch as a chair broke over fridge-guy's head, and the big man went down. The tall stranger still held the top of the ruined chair.

"Fun times," he said to Dawson with a grin, wading into the fray to clock an incoming biker with a punch that spun him around before he fell heavy on a table and broke it in half.

Grady and the redhead were surrounded by three men with knives. While the big men had bulk and muscle, Grady and his new friend were fast and wiry and clearly had martial arts training.

One of the giants swung a ham-sized fist at Grady's head. Grady went low, grabbed his arm, and pulled the guy across his back to land flat on the floor with a thud that shook the whole bar. Red had grabbed a full bottle of beer and wielded it like a cudgel to the back of one guy's head, then swept his feet out from under him as the biker stumbled.

The patrons who weren't hardcore HDF either fled while they had the chance or hung back to watch the fight.

A shotgun blast rang out, and Dawson flinched, expecting pain and blood.

"That's enough! Drop your weapons, or the next one doesn't miss." The bartender had a "fuck around and find out" glint in his eyes and a shotgun in his hands that had just put a hole through the dartboard.

Dawson laid his knife at his feet but wasn't about to reveal his hidden arsenal.

"Cops are on the way," the bartender announced. "So if any of y'all are on parole, got a court date coming up, or can't make bail, you'd best leave now."

Sirens outside made the threat real. Two men bolted for the back door, but three armed deputies came through the back as the sheriff and another officer entered, guns raised, from the front.

"What the fuck is going on?" Sheriff Rollins growled. He scowled when he saw the tall man and the redhead holding up badges.

"Agent Bartlett Gibson, Tennessee Bureau of Supernatural Investigation," the tall man said.

"Agent RJ Tucker, TBSI," the redhead echoed.

"Happened to be in the right place to stop an armed brawl," Gibson said smoothly, not appearing to notice how the fed badges made Rollins's eye twitch.

Interesting that he's not mentioning the HDF connection, Dawson thought. *Is that the case that brought them here?*

Gibson's nonchalance seemed to intensify the sheriff's ire as he turned his attention to Dawson and Grady.

"Why am I not surprised to find a couple of Kings in the thick of things? Why the hell are you here?" Rollins barked.

"Trying to find out who roofied Knox. This guy all but admitted it," Dawson added with a none-too-gentle "nudge" with his foot against one of the downed attackers, "and I'm betting one of their buddies snuck into the hospital to try to poison him."

"And in case you missed it, they're HDF assholes," Grady chimed in. Rollins looked ready to pop, although Dawson wasn't sure what part of the situation had him on the verge of losing his temper.

"Sheriff!" Everyone turned to look at Gibson. "How about you get these scumbags into custody and book them. I'm claiming jurisdiction. We'll be in touch."

Rollins opened his mouth to argue, then snapped it shut with murder in his eyes. He turned to the rowdy barflies. "All right you sons of bitches—hands in front of you, weapons down. Twitch the wrong way, and I'll taser your asses until you glow like Christmas lights."

"I'll handle the Kings," Gibson added. Rollins's eyebrows shot up, and Dawson thought the sheriff might have an aneurysm.

"Excuse me?"

"You heard me," Gibson replied, unperturbed. "I'll come down to your office with all the official paperwork. Thank you for the assist."

Dawson stifled a smug grin at Rollins's consternation, knowing he and Grady were going to feel the brunt of the angry sheriff's ire sooner or later. He cast a look at Gibson, unsure whether he and Grady were still in the frying pan or had jumped right into the flames.

Rollins and his deputies had the bar brawlers zip-tied and Mirandized in record time, herding them out to the waiting SUVs. Dawson and Grady edged closer to each other, trying to figure out how they fit into the messy puzzle.

Gibson turned to the bartender. "Those HDF guys come in here often?"

The bartender laid his shotgun on the bar. His thundering defiance had faded, leaving him just looking tired. "More than I'd like. They picked us, we didn't invite them. I keep watering down their beer, and the kitchen knows to burn or over-salt their food, but they won't take the hint."

"You know anything about their friend getting drugged?" Gibson asked, with a nod toward Dawson and Grady.

"Knox? I remember him coming in to handle a service call. He talked to the manager, and he fixed the dishwasher. The boss had to go log in a delivery, and I had some guy whose card kept getting declined. Knox didn't order anything except a soda when he first got here, and I didn't see him leave." He shrugged. "Figured he went out the kitchen door."

"Who reported the problem with the dishwasher? Who worked kitchen staff that day?" Tucker asked.

"Don't know without looking at the schedule, but I can find out," the bartender replied. He walked to a bulletin board just inside the kitchen doorway and came back a minute later.

"Carl Kaufman was the cook—he's been here for years. Good guy, keeps his head down," the bartender reported. "Bill Hammond was bussing. Twitchy little guy, only been here a couple of months. Sherry Owens waited tables. She's got no patience with that HDF crap."

"Where's Bill now?" Tucker eyed the kitchen doorway and reached for his gun.

"Not working tonight, but I can get you his address."

Gibson nodded, and the bartender gave him directions. "I had to drop him off one night because his car broke down," the barkeeper explained.

"If he shows up here, call me." Gibson handed the man his card and motioned for Dawson and Grady to follow him outside. The deputies were gone, and so were the rest of the customers—every car except for Denny's truck and the black 'Vette.

"Which of the Kings are you?" Gibson asked, looking from Dawson to Grady.

"I'm Dawson, and he's Grady."

"Pleased to meet you." Gibson shook their hands, and Tucker did the same. "You heard our introductions. Gotta say, I was surprised to see you here. Didn't figure it to be the kind of place to give you a warm welcome."

"Those assholes roofied Grady's brother and damn near killed him. They tried to make it look like an accident, and when the first time failed, they sent someone to the hospital to fuck with Knox's medications," Dawson replied.

"We got a tip that Knox came here the day he got drugged, so we thought we'd have a look for ourselves." Dawson grimaced. "And found a bunch of HDF sons of bitches. Christ—no wonder Knox almost got killed."

"So now we know who roofied him—but not who set him up or why," Grady chimed in. "That's why we're here. Why are you?"

An unspoken conversation seemed to pass between Gibson and Tucker, and Dawson guessed they were debating how much to say.

"Right now, I don't think our case is related to what you're working on," Gibson said. "So I'd rather not drag you in since it sounds like you've got enough on your plate. If that changes, we'll find you. And if you need us, call." He handed Dawson his card.

Dawson and Grady drove away before any of the bikers could come back with reinforcements. "What the hell do you think that was about?" Dawson asked when they had put enough distance between them and The Maverick to feel certain they hadn't been followed.

"Can you be more specific?" Grady snarked, nursing a split lip and what might be a black eye. "The bar fight or the feds?"

Dawson shifted in his seat, wincing at the shallow cuts that made his shirt stick to the drying blood. "I think the HDF part is pretty clear. I don't think the bar owner or the bartender was involved in drugging Knox. My bet is on the kitchen help—the new guy. Let's add his name to the ones Denny's hacker friend is looking into."

"He figured out that the dishwasher came from Knox's store and broke it on purpose? Why?"

Dawson shrugged. "Maybe the service call was legit, and something happened after Knox was there—he might have seen or overheard something. Or the kitchen guy *thought* Knox did and panicked."

"I don't get it. There've always been scum like the HDF and the SPS, but they used to stay in the shadows. Now, they're coming out of the woodwork," Grady replied. "What changed?"

"Cody and Max told us about how up in New York, the Alliance is investigating a trafficking ring that kidnapped shifters and people with special abilities. Steve and Kyle helped stop that warlock out in Boone who was part of some sort of witch network," Dawson mused, mentioning some of their hunter friends.

"Maybe that's shaken up the players enough for them to jockey for position. If a couple of people—or creatures—at the top got knocked off their thrones, everyone else tries to level up. And groups like the HDF and the SPS figure their targets are more vulnerable than usual, so they go for the kill," Grady finished for him.

"And that's without dragging the Syndicate into it," Dawson added. "Shit. This is getting so messy. I can't tell if we're the targets or the collateral damage."

Grady's phone buzzed, and he put the call on speaker. "Colt —what's up?"

"Knox is waking up. Denny's negotiating with the doctor to let him go home."

"How to say 'Denny doesn't think Knox is safe in the hospital' without actually saying that," Grady replied.

"Yeah. And it's not just Knox's safety—If someone's after him, then other people at the hospital could get hurt. We can protect him at Denny's."

Dawson heard the worry in Colt's voice. "Did something else happen?"

"No. But Denny and I have gotten some info—and I don't like what we're hearing." Colt paused. "How did it go at the bar?"

Dawson and Grady both laughed. "That's a whole 'nother story," Dawson replied. "And we made some new 'friends'—which opens up a different can of worms."

"Christ, can't let you two out of our sight," Colt fake-grumbled.

"Did you expect anything else?" Grady snarked.

"No, but I can hope. How did I end up being the responsible one?" Colt's question didn't sound entirely rhetorical.

"I don't know, but it's a scary thought," Dawson agreed. "We're on our way. See you in a few."

"Do you think any of this connects to what I found in Dad's journal?" Grady raised the question Dawson had been trying to avoid.

"I don't know. It would be bad enough on its own. Maybe Knox was just in the wrong place at the wrong time and heard something he shouldn't," Dawson replied, starting to feel the ache from the fight in every muscle.

"But the feds don't show up unless something big's going on. I can't remember the last time the TBSI stuck its nose into things around here. The Kings have had an understanding with them going back a long way. After all—we were here first," he finished.

They were quiet for a while, and Dawson grew pensive.

"Talk to me, Daw." Grady interrupted his thoughts. "I can tell when you're brooding."

Dawson sighed. "Did you ever have a memory that didn't seem important at the time, but when you look back on it, it means something completely different?"

Grady frowned. "Maybe. You mean like how watching Brendon Frasier's ass in *The Mummy* instead of Rachel Weisz's made me realize I was gay?"

Dawson chuckled. "Sorta like that. Except not as much fun." He grew silent again, trying to figure out how to put his thoughts into words.

"The summer before Mom and Dad died—I was almost seventeen. They didn't exactly hide conversations about bigger hunts, but they didn't go out of their way to let Colt, Knox, and me know about situations they thought were too dangerous," Dawson recalled.

"I was fourteen, so they didn't pull me in on anything harder than some easy hauntings," Grady replied.

"They mostly sent us on milk runs too—except for a couple that turned out to be more than they expected," Dawson agreed with a rueful chuckle.

"I don't know where the rest of you were, but I remember it being late at night, and maybe they thought I was watching a movie or in my room. Mom, Dad, and Uncle Denny were all talking in the kitchen about a dark witch who was helping the Syndicate. Curse coins, enhancing compulsive behavior like gambling, helping cover up crimes by blurring memories—that sort of thing."

"It would make sense for the Syndicate to have some witches in their pocket," Grady agreed. "They'd come in handy for those types of things—and more."

Dawson nodded. "At the time, I didn't think much of it. Just the grown-ups talking, you know? Not long after that, Mom and Dad were in the plane crash." He paused until the lump in his throat cleared. "I never heard that the witch was caught. Didn't think of it afterward, what with everything that happened. But now, I wonder if Denny suspected that the witch had something to do with the crash and steered me away from it."

"So did my dad stumble onto some unfinished business and pick up the case? He loved your dad like a brother, even if he was adopted. If he caught the scent of a hunt that might stop the person who killed your folks—"

"He could have gotten closer than he knew." Dawson didn't like where this line of thinking headed, but they didn't dare turn a blind eye.

"The werewolf fight that killed him—was that just a hunt that went bad, or did someone want to make sure he stopped poking around into the past?" Grady speculated.

"I think Denny knows more than he's let on. Maybe he's been protecting us, or maybe he hasn't put it all together, but I think we're overdue for a long talk," Dawson responded. "Knox and Colt should be part of it—they might have missing pieces and not even realize it."

When they got to the hospital, Dawson checked the parking lot for anything suspicious. He bristled at the sight of one of the sheriff's vehicles.

"What's Rollins doing here?" Dawson muttered.

"His job," Grady observed drily. "Aside from having it in for our family, he's a decent sheriff. He might be following up after the fight at The Maverick, or maybe he heard Knox was coming around and wanted to get a statement."

"Maybe," Dawson grudgingly admitted. He agreed that Rollins was a good sheriff with solid reasons to be perpetually annoyed at the Kings. But Rollins tended to rely on more conventional law enforcement sources and methods, even if he and much of his department were shifters. That left him constantly at loggerheads with Dawson's family, who focused on supernatural crimes and occult investigations.

They heard raised voices as soon as they got out of the elevator on Knox's floor.

"The boy is barely awake. Let him get his wits about him before you start grilling him," Denny challenged, blocking the door to what Dawson guessed was Knox's new room.

"Three questions—that's all. Hardly an interrogation. If he can't answer, I'll try later. But the first memories are often the truest. Less time to be influenced by seeing or hearing other things," Rollins argued.

"Are you saying we'd try to alter his testimony?" Denny sounded snappish, like he was running on fumes.

"Not on purpose. Come on, Denny. I'm trying to help. I don't have to get your permission—Knox is a grown-ass man. Don't make me barge in there just to do my job."

Denny gave the sheriff the stink eye and then stepped aside. "I don't like it, but I can see you're not going to go away until you get what you want. Three questions. That's it. If you need more, you come back when he's had a chance to recover."

"I want to catch whoever did this as much as you do," Rollins said. "We've got someone in custody—but I have a feeling they didn't come up with the idea themselves. If there's a whole lot of ugly about to bust loose, I want a heads-up."

Dawson and Grady hung back, waiting for the argument to be over before they followed Rollins and Denny into Knox's room. Colt stood beside Knox's bed, where a chair pulled up alongside made it clear he'd been keeping vigil.

Knox was sitting up in bed, and while he still wore a hospital gown and remained hooked up on a monitor, his color had improved, and the IV was gone.

"This isn't a good time," Colt said defensively, putting himself between Knox and the sheriff.

Knox drew him back by their clasped hands. "It's okay, Colt. I can do this."

"You just woke up," Colt muttered.

"A couple of hours ago. I know my name, what year it is, who's president, and I can count on my fingers," Knox said with fond patience. "It'll be all right."

"Three questions," Denny reminded the sheriff, who rolled his eyes.

"God, what is it with you Kings? Knox—glad to see you looking better," Rollins said.

"Lucky to be here," Knox replied. "But I'm still feeling peaked. Better ask me fast."

Dawson couldn't tell if Knox was manipulating the interview or telling the truth about his shaky recovery. *Maybe a little of both.*

"Did you see who drugged you?"

Knox shook his head. "No. Someone grabbed me from behind and jabbed me in the neck. It was 'lights out' before I hit the ground."

"Do you know anyone who has it out for you?" the sheriff asked.

Colt inched closer in support, and Knox gave his hand a squeeze. "I've done wrong by people, but I've tried to make up for it. That doesn't require anyone to forgive me, and I imagine some never will. I paid what I owed, and I left all that behind me. But I've got a theory."

Knox reached for a paper cup of water next to the bed, and Colt hurried to hand it to him. After he'd taken a few sips, he looked back to the sheriff.

"I went to The Maverick to fix the dishwasher we'd sold them a month ago. Never been there before. It wasn't a place I frequented back in the day, and I mostly stay out of bars now. I was alone in the kitchen, hunkered down in front of the machine, trying to reach a button on the inside. Would have been real easy for someone to over-look me," Knox added and paused for another sip.

"I heard two men talking outside the kitchen. Didn't see their faces and didn't care at the time. One man said, 'Gonna fuck those dogs up but good,' and the other said, 'make it look like teeth, and maybe the fangers will get the blame.'"

Fuck, Grady thought. *That had to be connected to those coyote shifter deaths. And a bar full of Human Defense Front crazies? Yeah—not suspicious at all. Right.*

"I was being quiet, but they must have noticed me then. It wouldn't have taken much to track me back to the hardware store— I'd driven a company van," Knox said. "Anyway, I went back to the shop to make sure payroll ran. I heard a noise out back, went to check, and two guys grabbed me and jabbed a needle in my neck. I woke up here. It could have been the same two guys I overheard at the bar. Again, I didn't catch their faces. Too many shadows. But one was taller than me, the other had broad shoulders like a swimmer."

Sheriff Rollins gave a curt nod, seeming to accept Knox's account. He pulled a photo from his jacket pocket. "Last question." He gave a pointed look at Denny. "Do you recognize this woman?"

He passed the photo to Grady, who held it for Knox. Knox squinted at the picture for a minute, studying the face, then shook his head.

"No. Not familiar at all. Who is she?"

Grady returned the picture, and Rollins pocketed it again. "We think she's the woman who impersonated a nurse and purposely gave you the wrong medication. She's an HDF supporter who seems to have gone on a long, sudden vacation without leaving a forwarding address," he added in a dry tone.

"Thank you for stopping in." Denny made it clear from his voice and body language that the interview was at an end. "Any chance those dead coyote shifters were killed by HDF folks?"

Rollins's eyes narrowed. "You know I can't comment on other investigations. And since you Kings have a lot on your plate, I'd suggest you leave the law to my deputies and me. Even if you do have a couple of friendly feds."

"Just being helpful, Sheriff," Denny replied with a twitch of a smile. "Let us know how we can help."

Rollins muttered something under his breath Dawson didn't quite catch and left. Colt eyed the door for a moment and then turned to them after Knox settled back in bed.

"While Knox was sleeping, I went over the room carefully," Colt said. "He's had nightmares. Maybe that's not a surprise after everything that happened, but I figured it pays to be careful. So I did a perimeter warding and a cleansing ritual, and when I went poking into every corner, I found a hex bag."

"Where is it?" Denny demanded, immediately concerned.

Colt shrugged. "I took a picture of it and then went outside to the smoking area and burned it. No telling how long it's been in the room, but I'm gonna bet someone left it for Knox. He hasn't had any nightmares since then."

He bent down and kissed Knox on the forehead. Knox smiled at him with more happiness than Dawson had seen on his face in a long time. Colt was good for Knox, and Dawson was glad they had found each other.

"Great. Now we've got witches involved," Denny muttered.

Grady shrugged. "Is it really a surprise? The HDF and the SPS probably both have witches on speed dial. I wonder if the feds have gotten more information since I don't think we're going to get a peep out of Rollins."

Dawson sighed. "I'll let the hardware store and the body shop know we'll be out for a couple more days. And after that hex bag, we need to make sure someone's with Knox at all times until we can move him home."

"I've got the doctor working up discharge papers," Denny replied. "That hex bag nonsense is the icing on the cake. Knox and Colt are safer at my place. Y'all can come too if you want. We'll hunker down and ward up."

"We'll keep digging and try to find out who's responsible so we can all go back to normal—well, 'King normal' anyhow," Dawson replied with a crooked smile.

Within the hour, Knox was in a wheelchair heading for the door. Colt pushed the chair, Dawson and Grady flanked him, and Denny led the way. They didn't draw their weapons, but everyone in town knew that the Kings hunted monsters and didn't do it barehanded.

To Dawson's relief, they got Knox and Colt into Denny's truck without incident. Dawson and Grady followed them home and stayed until Knox got settled.

"We're going to swing by the body shop and make sure everything's in order, up the wardings just in case, and then head home and do some research," Dawson said when they declined Denny's offer to stay for dinner. "There's got to be something that ties all this together."

Concern flickered in Denny's eyes. "Maybe this is one time you oughta leave it to the feds."

Dawson wanted to ask about links to the deaths of Grady's dad and granddad as well as his own father, but the time wasn't right. *Let's get Knox safe. Then we need to talk.*

"Nah. Can't let them have all the fun," Dawson countered with a smile he didn't feel. "We'll call to check in later tonight. Sooner if we find a hot lead."

He and Grady were quiet on the ride back to their house. "I hope you didn't mind," Dawson said. "I just needed some time for us alone, after everything. Even if we spend it researching the case."

Grady reached over and put a hand on Dawson's thigh. "Knowing Knox is safer at Denny's takes a big weight off my shoulders. But I'm happy to have 'us' time before things get crazy again."

"How about I put that frozen chicken tetrazzini in the oven and make a salad, and you can tell me all about the honeymoon trip ideas you've got in that folder on your laptop?" Dawson joked.

"You weren't supposed to look in there!" Grady blushed.

"It wasn't marked 'secret.' Or weren't you planning on taking me with you?" Dawson teased, loving Grady's reaction.

"Of course you're *coming* with me," Grady replied. "But that folder's just a bunch of random things—probably mostly trash."

Dawson shrugged. "After all the serious stuff, I might like to look at 'trash' as long as I'm with you. I've got some other ideas for honeymoon trip activities we can try out later." He waggled his eyebrows with exaggerated lechery and felt rewarded by Grady's laugh.

"I'll definitely take you up on that!" Grady promised, giving his leg a squeeze. "Practice makes perfect, after all."

4

GRADY

"I THINK I FOUND SOMETHING." GRADY LOOKED UP FROM HIS LAPTOP. He was still stuffed from dinner, and his heart felt full after their discussion of places for a someday honeymoon.

Dawson's comments were pretty much what Grady expected— nowhere haunted or with a dark history and preferably a place with good food, a nice view, and comfy beds.

If we ever catch a break with the hunting, we can afford to go somewhere farther away. The beach? Disney World? Vegas and New York City would be nice vacations, but not honeymoon material. Maybe a cozy cabin on a lake—or a private little beach bungalow at the Outer Banks.

"What's up?" Dawson brought Grady a cold beer before he settled on the other side of the sturdy farm-style kitchen table. The dishes were done and leftovers put away, but the whole house still smelled like dinner.

"Ever heard of the Kirkland Bushwhackers?" Grady asked.

"Anything like tally whackers?" Dawson managed a playfully lascivious grin.

"Not everything's about sex."

"Don't blow my illusions to smithereens."

Grady countered with a sinful smile of his own. "Oh, I'll 'blow'

67

you alright—later. But first...Bushwhackers."

Dawson gave an exaggerated sigh and came around to look over Grady's shoulder. Grady tried valiantly to ignore his nearness, the smell of his shampoo, and the hint of cologne that made their evening at home feel a little more like date night.

"The Kirkland Bushwhackers were a gang of Army deserters during the Civil War. They preyed on travelers, and while they had a particular hatred of Union soldiers, they also killed Confederates who were traveling with anything valuable," Grady recounted.

"Lovely. And do they haunt somewhere? Because I don't imagine they want to move on to their final reward."

"There have been legends for over a century that the Bush-whackers still patrol their old territory," Grady replied. "The stories vary—"

"Don't they always?"

Grady ignored the snark. "But the ghost attacks seem to be worse some years than others. This year, they are higher than usual."

"How come we haven't heard about this before?" Dawson set down his half-empty beer bottle and started to knead Grady's shoulders. Grady leaned back into the touch and moaned in pleasure as Dawson's fingers worked tight muscles loose.

"I've got other ideas on what might make you sound like that," Dawson said, leaning close to Grady's ear.

"And I'll take you up on it—once I show you what I found," Grady said, knowing they would both feel rewarded at the end.

"The Bushwhackers' ghosts supposedly come back for three out of ten years—no idea why. But if that's true, it explains why we didn't hear much about them. We were probably too young to be involved the last time," Grady told him.

"And now?"

Grady turned the computer so Dawson could see better. "Three bikers—presumably human—were found dead on one of the roads that the Kirkland Gang used to patrol. The report says they appeared to have been 'mauled by animals.'"

"Fuck," Dawson muttered. "No telling what actually killed them.

But since it might be a malicious haunting, you can bet the HDF will use it to try to start a panic."

"I'm thinking that we might want to take a drive up there tomorrow and see for ourselves. If it's a run-of-the-mill black shuck or were-critter, we can take care of it. My suspicion is that the 'cycles' were something people made up whenever anything odd happened."

"Sounds like a plan to me. Do we know if the bikers were HDF or SPS? Because that could make a big difference in whether we run into unwanted company." Dawson took the last drops from his bottle and picked up Grady's empty as well.

"That certainly wasn't anything mentioned in the news report." Grady shut down his laptop after he'd saved everything they would need for their trip. "I sent the bikers' names to one of our hacker friends—they should be able to find out if the dead guys were involved in either of those groups."

"Like we don't have enough trouble with monsters—crazy people don't make things any easier," Dawson said.

Grady came up behind him at the kitchen sink and gripped Dawson's hips, bucking against him a couple of times before sliding a hand around to cup his package. "Research is done. Time for those rewards," he murmured, blowing against the back of Dawson's neck, gratified when it raised goosebumps.

"Already ahead of you. Everything's ready."

While Grady had finished his research, Dawson had set up for movie night in the living room with a huge bowl of popcorn, a bucket of cold beers, and one of their favorite superhero movies already queued on streaming. They had both changed into sweatpants and T-shirts before dinner, and Grady loved the way Dawson's arousal tented the gray material with a promise for later.

They snuggled close on the oversized couch, and Dawson started the movie, turning off the lamp so the room was lit only by the TV's glow. Grady leaned up to kiss him, slow and lingering, tasting beer and garlic and something completely Dawson.

"You're going to miss the movie," Dawson joked.

"That's the idea." Grady kissed him again with intention as his hand slid lower to tease around the waistband of Dawson's pants before dipping inside.

"Looks like you're ready for the *coming* attractions," Grady continued.

"How do you want it?" Dawson breathed as Grady wrapped a hand around his cock and made a couple of slow pulls.

"I want to blow you while you suck me," Grady murmured. "And then...we can make it up as we go along."

They shucked off their clothing, movie forgotten, and rearranged themselves to lie toe-to-head on the broad couch. Grady nuzzled Dawson's happy trail, content with a face full of wiry hair and the overwhelming scent of his lover's arousal. He cupped Dawson's ass and drew him closer, licking and lightly nipping along his thighs as his hands roamed.

Dawson pulled Grady's groin close and swallowed his hard cock in one move. He slid a finger between Grady's cheeks and teased at his hole, promising more.

Before he lost himself entirely to sensation, Grady toyed with the head of Dawson's stiff prick, wetting his lips with the pre-come and savoring the taste before he licked up and down with the flat of his tongue. That drew a very interested moan from Dawson, and Grady smiled as he bobbed and licked the thick cock, flicking his tongue through the slit and adding the barest scrape of teeth as he pulled up the shaft.

All the tension of the past few days meant that neither of them were likely to last long. Grady knew they both needed the release as well as confirmation of their bond.

"Come on, Daw. Let go," he urged, and Dawson gasped and arched. Grady swallowed every drop only seconds before his own climax rushed through him, losing himself in the warm heat of his lover's mouth.

He licked and sucked Dawson's cock as he trembled with after-shocks. Grady loved being able to drive Dawson wild with pleasure, and he felt boneless and relaxed after his orgasm.

When he finally felt able to move, Grady managed to sit up and searched for his discarded pants and shirt. He clicked off the TV and carried the food out to the kitchen while Dawson gathered his things before they shuffled to bed, planning to clean up the rest in the morning.

"Sorry that date night wasn't more exciting," Dawson said as they crawled under the covers. "I'm just happy to be with you, Gray."

"Are you apologizing for toe-curling sex? Because I'm very happy —unless you're offering a do-over, which I'd totally take you up on," Grady replied, barely stifling a yawn.

"Tomorrow," Dawson answered, his voice gravelly from deep throating Grady's cock. "We can start the day right before we go looking for your tally whackers."

"Bushwhackers."

"Only if they're straight."

"You're impossible," Grady sighed at the bad pun.

"Yep. But I'm yours."

Grady leaned forward to kiss him. "And I'm yours. Forever."

———

THE NEXT MORNING, AFTER A SATISFYING ROUND TWO, DAWSON AND Grady headed for the place where the bikers' bodies were found. The Mustang roared along the twisty mountain roads, hugging the curves and opening up wide in the straightaways. Grady laughed when they caught air on a bump, and Dawson turned the radio up loud.

Dawson had the windows open, and the air ruffled his dark hair. For the first time in weeks, Grady felt free of the overwhelming certainty that something bad was going to happen. He knew that feeling wouldn't—couldn't—last, but he intended to enjoy every second while it did.

A mile before they reached the murder site, Dawson slowed the car and turned down the radio. Grady felt the lighthearted mood slip away.

"I'm not sure what we're going to find—or who else might be looking," Dawson cautioned. "So stay sharp."

The police tape was gone, but trampled grass and ominous dark stains made it simple for them to find the right spot.

"Not enough blood," Grady muttered. "This was just the dumping spot—whoever killed them wanted the bodies found."

Dawson nodded. "Yeah. This stretch of road isn't a superhighway, but it's still got traffic. Too much for a creature—normal or not—to rip three men to shreds."

The EMF reader remained silent, ruling out ghosts. They searched the tall grass and nearby ditch for nearly an hour, but if any clues had been there, they were gone now.

"Feel like a hike?" Dawson asked.

They had come prepared to walk the nearby woods. Dawson found a side road where he pulled the Mustang off onto the shoulder, and they grabbed their weapons and a gear bag, then headed into the forest.

"Been a long time since we've gone hiking when we weren't looking for bodies or monsters," Grady mused.

"We do so much of this for the cases, I didn't think you'd want to hike in our free time. What's Uncle Denny call it—a 'busman's holiday'?"

Grady shrugged. "We could always go somewhere that we haven't worked cases. There are some really pretty spots."

"With our luck, we'd still find ghosts and monsters. But maybe if we went to one of the more touristy parks, we'd be less likely to run into trouble," Dawson agreed. "We could make an overnight out of it, see a movie, try out a local steakhouse."

Grady smiled. "That sounds nice. I'd like that. Once things slow down." He felt grateful that Dawson didn't point out that it didn't seem like things *ever* settled for them.

"Some of the guys at the garage hike. I can ask which trails—and restaurants—are their favorites," Dawson volunteered. "Since you've been doing all the honeymoon research," he added. His teasing tone didn't hide the fond smile.

Grady had always found it soothing to be out in nature—when they weren't in the middle of a hunt. The mountains and forest were beautiful, and he could almost imagine hearing a faint, far-off song coming from the hills themselves.

"Still think the mountains sing to you?" Dawson teased, guessing Grady's thoughts. Grady had confided that image years ago, and Dawson remembered with fond skepticism.

"You're just jealous because you can't hear them," he joked. "And for your information, it's not all the mountains. The feeling's stronger some places than others. And not all of the songs are nice." He shuddered. "I try to avoid those spots."

Dawson ruffled Grady's hair. "You are such a geek. Are you going to start twirling in a meadow like that old Julie Andrews movie?"

Grady gave him a look. "No. And I'm not going to burst into song either. In case you wondered."

They fell back into hunting mode, alert to everything around them. The EMF reader in Grady's pocket stayed silent, but he couldn't shake the feeling that settled over him the deeper they went into this stretch of woods.

Usually, he felt peaceful in the forest. Now, restlessness had him on high alert, and despite the bright sun, the area had an ominous presence.

Places have spirits, Grady thought. *Genius loci. Daemons. Most of them are good. But some...* Grady knew that the tribes that first settled these mountains considered certain areas to be places of good fortune and safety and that other locations were avoided as unlucky or cursed.

Privately, Grady had always wondered whether those spirits had anything to do with the "songs" he heard. He'd tried more than once to look up that sort of psychic phenomenon and hadn't found much. Nothing as well-documented as the kind of visions Dawson got. *I'm a Richardson by blood, so any abilities in the King line wouldn't apply to me.*

Grady was just fine with chalking the songs up to his imagination. Now, he wondered if his jitters had anything to do with its violent history.

All those people the Bushwhackers killed left a resonance behind. Even if the ghosts didn't stick around, violence leaves a stain on the land.

Dawson bumped his shoulder and motioned for Grady to follow. They used hand signals on hunts to avoid revealing their location or plans, and the gestures had become a second language.

Grady drew his gun and checked for threats while Dawson led the way up a rocky incline. Near the top, Grady saw what Dawson had spotted—a shallow cave that looked like it might have been the lair of some creature.

"Doesn't look recent." Grady peered inside. "Doesn't smell like something's just been here, either."

Dawson shook his head. "I thought maybe if the bikers really were attacked by some sort of cryptid it might have a den somewhere, but this isn't it."

They hiked for another hour, covering the area close to where the bodies were found. Both men had been raised to have good outdoor skills and trained to be trackers—essentials given the thickly wooded territory in Western North Carolina where the Kings made their home.

Grady didn't see any evidence of a large predator—no tracks, tufts of fur, or droppings. *A normal animal kills to eat or to protect itself or its young. It doesn't just leave torn up bodies next to a road.*

"Might as well head back," Dawson said, and they trekked to the car in silence. Remaining vigilant had kept them from enjoying the walk for its own sake. Not finding evidence made the effort feel like a waste of time.

"Uh-oh," Grady murmured as they neared the Mustang. A black pickup had pulled in front of the sports car, and four large men appeared to be waiting for them.

"Shit." Dawson's gun was already in hand from prowling the woods.

Grady couldn't interpret the strangers' presence as anything but dangerous. Still, firing on humans without provocation went against everything he believed.

A rifle shot splintered the trunk of a sapling near Dawson's head. Both men dropped and rolled to avoid presenting an easy target.

"The next one won't miss," a man's voice shouted. "Come on out, and let's have a little chat."

Grady knew they could run, only to be hunted through unfamiliar woods. With the Mustang held hostage, they weren't leaving, and this stretch of isolated road didn't have houses or towns in sight.

"We can hear you just fine from here," Dawson shouted back, gun cocked and ready. Neither he nor Grady moved closer to the road. "What's on your mind?"

Another crack of the rifle, and Grady cried out as a shot grazed his upper arm. He clapped a hand to cover the wound and belly crawled to denser cover as Dawson opened fire on their attackers.

Dawson's first shot struck the rifleman in the shoulder, putting him out of the game. The men fired back, narrowly missing them. Grady gritted his teeth, glad it was his left arm that was injured. He rose just far enough to see and aimed for the knees. Two went down writhing on the ground and clutching their injured legs.

Grady heard Dawson squeeze off another shot, and the remaining gunman staggered, clutching his right arm as he sagged against the truck. Dawson's last bullet flattened the front tire of the pickup.

"Toss your guns into the ditch," Dawson shouted before breaking cover. "All of them. If I see you twitch, I'll shoot to kill."

He glanced toward Grady's hiding place. "You okay?"

Grady could hear the worry in his lover's voice. "I'll live."

Once the weapons were out of the way, Dawson walked toward the road, with Grady close behind him. Warm blood ran down the inside of Grady's sleeve, and his arm hurt like a son of a bitch. He could still move his hand, and the blood wasn't flowing fast enough to be a worry, so he figured he'd be okay for a little while longer.

"Cover me," Dawson told Grady and pulled zip ties from his pocket.

"Face down, hands behind your backs. Play nice, and we'll call for help before you bleed out. Try something stupid, and we'll leave you to the coyotes. Got a feeling they have a score to settle with you folks anyhow," Dawson continued. Grady followed his gaze to the HDF patches on their prisoners' jackets and remembered the murdered coyote shifters.

Once their attackers were tied at wrists and ankles, Dawson took off his overshirt and wrapped it around his hand before he gathered the guns from the ditch, careful not to touch them with bare skin. He loaded the weapons into the bed of the strangers' truck and turned back to the men on the ground.

"How'd you know we were here?" Dawson asked, holding his gun on them. Grady kept his Sig Sauer trained on the men, unwilling to take any chances. His arm throbbed.

"We figured Kings would show up, so we had a camera in the trees so we could watch and stay out of sight," one of the men answered. "And sure enough, there you were."

"Yeah, that didn't work out quite how you expected, did it?" Dawson's voice held barely contained anger, and Grady knew some of that fury came from worry about him.

Without ever turning his back or taking his eyes off the prisoners, Dawson stepped closer to Grady. "How bad?"

"A graze. Maybe stitches. Hurts like a mofo, but I've had worse." Grady jerked his head toward the captives. "What about them?"

Dawson pulled out his phone and thumbed a contact. "Hey, Gibson? We've got a present for you, all tied up and ready to go," he said to the fed. Grady listened as Dawson gave directions and gathered that they'd have backup shortly.

"Local sheriff's not going to be happy handing these idiots over to the feds," Grady observed.

"For all we know, the local sheriff's one of them," Dawson countered. "Hell, for as little as he's managed to do about what's going on, maybe our own sheriff is Supernatural Protection Society."

A shifter sheriff and deputies might find themselves sympathetic to the SPS, especially with the Human Defense Front stirring up dangerous trouble. While Grady thought Sheriff Rollins was biased about the Kings, he didn't like the idea of him being corrupt.

"Keep your eyes on them. I'm going to have a look at that arm." Dawson gently tugged at the rip in Grady's jacket sleeve where the bullet had torn its way clear.

"You're right. A graze. Not a through-and-through, so there's that, but fuck, it looks painful," Dawson said. He went to the Mustang and grabbed the first aid kit out of the back.

"This'll help slow the bleeding until I can get you fixed up proper," Dawson told him, wrapping the wound with gauze. Grady read the worry and protectiveness in his voice for the love it sprang from.

"I'll be fine. Just don't let those bastards get the drop on you. I don't trust them—they're still breathing." Grady made his voice loud enough on that last sentence for the downed men to hear him.

"Guess I'd better make sure they don't bleed out before they can stand trial." Dawson eyed their prisoners.

"Probably, although they don't deserve it," Grady agreed. "I've got your back." He lifted his gun to underscore his comment.

"Any of them moves, shoot to kill," Dawson told him. He turned toward their attackers. "You think you're going to try something? Fuck around and find out. Grady doesn't miss. Give me a hard time, and I'll let you bleed. Lie nice and still, and I'll wrap you up so you make it to a hospital with some of the blood on the inside."

Dawson made quick work of battlefield first aid. "That should hold you—just don't move around much. I'm not doing it a second time."

Gibson and Tucker rolled up in the black Corvette half an hour later, making Grady wonder where they'd been staying. Certainly not Asheville, and not even Kingston. That made him think their attackers weren't the only ones watching where the biker bodies had been dumped, waiting to see who showed up.

Bartlett Gibson unfolded his long, lanky frame from the 'Vette and sauntered toward them. Tucker walked beside him, completely in sync. Grady wondered how long they had been partners to get that sort of shared rhythm and whether they were partnered in other ways as well.

"I see you've already collected the trash," Gibson observed, looking at the zip-tied prisoners.

"Against my better judgment, they're still kicking," Dawson replied with a shrug. "Gift-wrapped for you to deliver to Gitmo or wherever."

"Tempting," Tucker said. "HDF is a hate group and a terrorist organization. We could rendition them to a black site, and no one would ever miss them."

Grady wasn't sure whether the two feds were role-playing to frighten the prisoners, but their words got a quick reaction.

"We didn't hurt nobody," one of the men argued, although he kept his position on the ground. "They jumped us."

"They shot Grady," Dawson pointed out in a tone that made it clear he'd pushed the boundaries of his patience by leaving the shooter breathing. "And they opened fire on us."

"I don't doubt it," Gibson replied. "Don't worry—we're not going to turn them over to the local sheriff. He's either in cahoots or inept—maybe both. They'll go to a federal facility where we can take our time getting acquainted." His smile showed teeth.

"You gonna get us all in that fancy car?" one of the other prisoners taunted.

"Nope. Got a couple of ambulances on their way, and the US Marshals will take over at the hospital, keeping you company until they can escort you to secure facilities," Gibson replied.

"We won't stop," the rifleman retorted. "There are more where we came from—a lot more. We got to one of the Kings—we can get to the rest of those freak-protecting assholes."

Grady felt his stomach curdle at the admission. *They hurt Knox, and they're proud of it.*

Sirens sounded in the distance. "That's your cue to get out of here," Gibson said to Dawson and Grady. "I'll call you when things settle down. We definitely need to talk."

Dawson and Grady hurried to the Mustang and were gone before the ambulances arrived. Once they were back on the road, Dawson gave Grady a worried once-over, eyeing the gauze where blood had seeped through. "You need a hospital?"

Grady shook his head. "They've got to report gunshot wounds, remember? Doc Smith can patch me. He's stitched me up from getting clawed by a black shuck—this isn't as deep."

Dawson's pained expression made it clear that he remembered

that hunt—and how quickly it had gone bad. The day certainly wasn't one of Grady's favorite memories either.

"Don't joke about that. You almost died."

Grady reached for his hand. "But I didn't."

"It was closer than I want to remember," Dawson muttered.

"So what do you make of our new fed friends?" Grady asked to shift the conversation, and his partner went along with the topic change.

"They came when I called, which counts for something. The local sheriff, or at least some of his people, are sympathizers with the HDF if not outright members," Dawson said. "The HDF sells a good sob story—poor pitiful humans being overwhelmed by dangerous supernatural predators. Might not work elsewhere, but people in these mountains already know that the things that go bump in the night are real."

"This 'eye for an eye' stuff just escalates," Grady worried aloud. "The HDF retaliates because something paranormal killed humans. Then the SPS takes revenge because humans killed supernatural creatures. There's no winning."

Dawson nodded, looking tired now that the adrenaline from the fight had faded. "I saw an old movie once that said the only way to win was to refuse to play. I think it's too late for that—so we need a Plan B."

Grady let Dawson fuss over him, calling "Doc Smith" from the road so he would be expecting them and later hovering as the retired doctor cleaned the bullet graze and dressed the wound.

"You're lucky it wasn't an inch to the right," Dr. Smith said as he peeled off his latex gloves. "Bullet hits the bone; it gets nasty. As it is, you should heal up fine, maybe not even much of a scar. Keep it clean and dry, watch out for infection, and try not to wave your arm around until the gash closes up."

Dawson's phone buzzed as they headed back to the Mustang. Grady felt the weight of the day's events and wanted nothing more than a good burger and a warm bed.

"You boys up to talking?" Gibson asked as Dawson held the

phone so Grady could hear. "We'll spring for takeout, so we can eat while we get caught up. We're staying at Overlook Cabins—number twenty-four. Seven o'clock?"

"You're pretty damn sure we'll show up," Dawson growled, and Grady knew that the day wore hard on him too.

"Figured you'd want to know what we got back from our sources —and forensics," Gibson returned easily, unflustered by Dawson's pique. "And we've got a few questions of our own. But I think you'll be very interested in what we've found." To the agent's credit, he didn't sound smug.

Dawson glanced to Grady, who nodded. "Okay. We'll be there. We've picked up on a few things ourselves." He ended the call and let out a long breath. "I'm sorry. You don't need that on top of everything," he said to Grady.

Grady shrugged, then winced when the motion made his arm ache. "We needed to eat anyhow. And maybe Gibson and Tucker got good intel with all their fancy connections. I'll call Denny and see what his network has turned up. I'd put our friends up against Gibson's government resources any day."

"And you'd probably be right," Dawson agreed. "But maybe if we put what we've gotten together, we'll figure out what's really happening. Because I've got the awful feeling that we're not seeing the whole picture."

They had time to go home, shower and change before meeting the agents. Dawson fussed over Grady and made sure the dressing on his arm didn't get wet. They stole a few moments of peace over coffee and cookies before heading out again.

"You sure you're up to going out?" Dawson asked. His concern warmed Grady even as it made him a little twitchy.

"Yeah—we don't have to make a late night of it. Eat food, swap info, come home. Good thing we started the morning off right, because I don't think there'll be much left of me by the time we get to bed," Grady replied.

"Eat another cookie. The sugar will help." Dawson pushed the plate closer to Grady.

"Already had two. I need to be able to make an attempt at eating whatever they're ordering for us," Grady protested.

"Hope it's good. I'm starving." Dawson grabbed a six-pack of beer to take with them as a gesture of goodwill, and they headed out.

———

OVERLOOK CABINS WERE PART OF A MOM-AND-POP MOTEL COMPLEX with a retro fifties vibe and enough modern upfits to be trendy. They parked the Mustang next to the black Corvette just as Gibson opened the door.

"Come in. The food just got here." He stepped aside to let them enter, and Grady breathed in the aroma of wood-smoked barbecue.

"Hope you like it. The guy at the front office told us where the locals eat." Tucker stood to welcome them.

The cabin had a kitchen with a table and a comfortable living room. A hallway in the back presumably went to one or more bedrooms. It felt cozy. The pine-paneled walls, plaid throws on the couch, and stuffed deer head on the wall retained the "rustic" vibe.

Dawson and Grady helped set out a feast of pulled pork, baked beans, potato salad, coleslaw, and cornbread on the counter as Gibson got out plates and Tucker set a bottle of beer at each place setting.

"Eat first—talk shop after," Gibson said, settling his lanky body into a chair beside Tucker, who didn't seem to mind the invasion of his space.

Dawson and Grady sat across from the pair, and Grady didn't feel self-conscious at all with his knee pressed against Dawson's under the table.

"If this tastes as good as it looks, I'll need to go for a run to work it off," Tucker said, although that hadn't stopped him from mounding his plate with food.

"I could make you chase the 'Vette," Gibson teased. "Be your pace car."

"I'd be drifting the whole way," Tucker joked back, trading stock car racing terms in their jibes.

Grady couldn't help trying to figure out their hosts. Gibson looked like he could be by the books. Every time Grady had seen the two agents on the clock, Gibson's shirt had been neatly pressed, tucked into his regulation khaki pants, hair just so, with manicured stubble.

Tucker, on the other hand, looked like chaos incarnate. He had a shaggy shock of red hair and a scruffy beard. Tucker's slightly rumpled clothing looked like he'd grabbed what he'd worn the previous day without bothering to iron.

"How did you two team up?" Dawson asked an instant before Grady could ask the same thing.

The lawmen exchanged a look.

"Now there's a story," Tucker said.

Gibson took a pull from his beer. "After the fourth time I arrested him, the powers that be decided we could either work together or spend the next decade chasing each other."

"Arrested?" Grady hadn't expected that.

"Ricky Jon—"

"RJ," Tucker interrupted, although Grady didn't think he minded as much as he pretended to.

"RJ," Gibson amended, "is a psychic—and until I straightened him out, a damn good con man."

"Yeah, you *straightened me out*. Let's go with that," Tucker snorted.

Gibson gave him a look. "Are you telling this story or am I?"

Tucker gave a royal wave and gulped his beer. "By all means. Continue."

Gibson rolled his eyes, and Grady glimpsed sly humor behind his all-business facade. "I'm a witch—mainly necromancy, but I have some other handy skills as well. That's how I ended up with the Tennessee Bureau of Supernatural Investigation. Given Tucker's talents, and his penchant for escaping, my bosses made him a deal. Join the team, stay clean, and his record gets erased."

"Wasn't there an old TV show like that?" Dawson joked. "I think

I've caught Uncle Denny watching re-runs late night."

"Several," Gibson deadpanned. "Everyone figured out what we already knew—we worked better when we were on the same side. Although he did lead me on a merry chase," he admitted with a grin.

"I let him chase me until I caught him," Tucker supplied with a knowing wink. "I get visions, and he sees dead people. Good partnership."

"You're a necromancer," Dawson repeated, stuck on something Gibson said a few minutes before. "So why don't you just bring the murder victims back to life and ask who killed them?"

Gibson grimaced. "Yeah, no. For one thing—that's not as easy as it sounds. And even if I did—assuming I could—what comes back isn't always the same. People don't see their killer if they're shot from a distance or attacked from behind. They might not know who had it in for them—you'd be surprised how often someone is surprised to wind up dead. Ghosts are very unreliable witnesses."

"Do your visions help prevent crimes or catch the perps?" Grady turned to Tucker.

"Sometimes. I can get images from a crime scene that can steer us in the right direction, or I'll get a warning that we're walking into a trap. Unfortunately, it's not as simple as on TV. I don't just go into a trance and see the murderer. And even if I did, it wouldn't be admissible evidence. We'd still have to prove it the old-fashioned way."

"I don't raise the dead—but I can usually summon their ghosts. They can be chatty and helpful, even if they aren't aware that what they know is valuable," Gibson jumped in.

"Did you get much from the bikers' ghosts?" Grady asked. "I'm assuming you've talked with them."

Gibson drained his beer and set the bottle aside. "Not everyone who dies hangs around afterward. Two of the souls had already departed by the time we got to the scene. The other remembered his name and knew he was dead. He didn't get a good look at what clawed him up, except that it was 'big as a man' and had yellow eyes."

Grady and Dawson exchanged a glance. "Sounds like some type of were-creature. Wolf or a big cat, maybe?"

Gibson nodded. "That's our theory. But the supernatural forensics came back with an interesting tidbit—traces of magic. Found the same thing with those dead coyote shifters."

"Magic?" Dawson leaned forward. "What kind?"

"We think it was a binding or a tracking spell," Tucker replied. "Which raises the question—who's the witch, and why were they involved?"

"We don't have a forensics team, but we've got friends who are pretty good at digging up answers," Dawson said. "Those guys at the bar who attacked us had rap sheets a mile long—most of it anti-cryptid bullshit and violent humans-only groups, plus assault, weapons violations, and petty crimes."

"Knox thinks someone realized he overheard their plans to make trouble and decided to shut him up permanently," Grady said, recounting what they had learned from his brother. "The fake nurse also had HDF ties and a revoked license. As far as anyone could find with the coyotes, they got in trouble with their pack, went out on their own, had some minor shady dealings, and ended up in the wrong place at the wrong time." He didn't credit Denny's hacker friends as the source of the information.

Gibson and Tucker nodded. "That matches what we've turned up. Someone wanted to send a message, so they killed the coyote shifters —and probably the bikers too," Gibson said.

"Since the stories of the bushwhacker ghosts never had them clawing people to shreds, we think whoever is behind all this co-opted the legend to give themselves cover," Tucker continued the thought.

"You think the same witch was involved with both?" Dawson echoed. "Playing for both teams?"

"Not just playing—possibly running the show," Gibson answered. "Ophelia Locklear has been involved with the vampire side of the Syndicate for a very long time. She may be a vampire herself or some other type of immortal. We think she's using the HDF and SPS as pawns—we're just not sure what her game is."

Gibson's words sent a shiver of ice down Grady's spine. "How long? More than thirty years?" He ignored Dawson's speculative gaze for the moment.

"Maybe. Why?" Gibson replied, eyes narrowing.

"My grandfather, Frank Richardson, was a hunter. I'm still trying to piece together what happened, but what I know for sure is that he and his wife were killed in a fire or explosion. His son, my father Aaron, was adopted by Michael King—Dawson's grandfather," Grady recounted. "Then years later, Dawson's parents were killed in a suspicious plane crash, and less than a year ago, Dad was killed in a werewolf hunt that wasn't a standard hunt. And just now, there have been two attempts on Knox's life."

"You think someone—possibly a witch—might have orchestrated all of that?" Tucker looked skeptical.

Grady shrugged. "I'm just now finding evidence that makes me wonder."

Gibson's expression suggested he was mulling over the possibility. "That would require stringing together a lot of 'ifs' and 'maybes,' but it would all depend on the 'why.' Given that the Kings have been hunting monsters in these parts for more than two hundred years, the family certainly has enemies. But to carry out a vendetta across three generations—there has to be a good reason."

"And that's what we don't know—yet," Dawson supplied. "I've got a theory that Frank and his wife were killed because they were on the trail of someone important. That ended the investigation. But what if my parents somehow picked up the trail decades later?"

"And what if my dad did the same, seven years after Ethan and Jackie died?" Grady put in. "They might not have even been looking for a connection—maybe they happened upon a related case or discovered the link by accident. Someone might have been tempted to make the 'King problem' go away—permanently."

"So of course you two are tempting fate yourselves by carrying on the tradition," Tucker observed.

"It's in our blood," Dawson said with a shrug.

"If someone's willing to kill for it, whatever was going on back then must still be happening," Grady speculated. "Otherwise, why make the effort? The damnedest thing is that none of our cases lately have been unusual or particularly important. Hauntings, feral creatures, a few curses—nothing significant."

"Unless—assuming there's one person throughout all this time doing the killing—you don't realize the connection, but the killer thinks you know," Tucker said.

Grady felt Tucker's words like a seismic shift in his brain. "Shit. You might be right."

"Maybe we can work our way from the ends to the middle if we collaborate," Gibson suggested. "You follow the clues from your family history, the way you'd handle any hunt, focusing on finding who killed the bikers and coyotes and how that might relate to what happened to Knox. We'll track our Syndicate leads and figure out if there's a big picture view we've been missing."

Dawson and Grady shared a wary glance.

"Sounds good," Grady replied, "on one condition—you share what you find with us just as completely as you want us to share with you."

"Deal," Gibson replied.

Grady couldn't stifle his yawn as his body warned it was time to crash.

"We've had quite a day, and Gray got shot. Thanks for the barbecue and intel, but I think it's time for us to go." Dawson stood, and they helped carry out the empties and shook hands with Gibson and Tucker.

"You have my number," Gibson told Dawson. "Text me Grady's, and I'll text you Tucker's. That way we can connect when something happens."

"Will do," Dawson agreed. He rested his hand on the small of Grady's back as they walked toward the door.

"And Grady? If you're right about the connections, you two better keep your heads down and watch your backs. Anyone capable of that kind of dark magic over all those years is a formidable enemy. You definitely don't want to run into them in a dark alley," Tucker warned.

"Agreed," Grady replied. "We'll be in touch."

5

DAWSON

"THESE ARE THE PROTECTIVE AMULETS I TOLD YOU ABOUT." DENNY held out two cloth drawstring pouches, one for Dawson and one for Grady. "I had them made by a root worker I know down in Charleston. Got some for Colt, Knox, and me too. Like I said, I was going to give them to you for Christmas but seems like you need them now so —'tis the season."

Angel wagged and wove in and out between their legs, then sat down and looked at them expectantly for treats. Dawson reached into his pocket for the dog biscuits he always carried, and Angel padded off with her spoils to enjoy them by the couch.

Dawson opened the pouch and removed a silver medallion covered with sigils and another small bag tied off with odd string.

"The necklace has protective markings from several cultures, and it's been blessed," Denny told them. "The other is a mojo bag. Don't open it; keep it in your pocket at all times, and occasionally feed it a couple of drops of blood and alcohol."

"Feed?" Grady's eyes widened, and he regarded the bag with suspicion.

Denny shrugged. "Each bag is said to have a protective presence inside. Can't say I understand exactly, but I know it's real and powerful—and you boys can use all the help you can get."

"Thanks," Grady said, putting the necklace on and slipping the bag into the pocket of his jeans as Dawson did the same. They had stopped by to drop off groceries since Denny was busy strengthening the wardings around the house.

"How's Knox?" Dawson asked as he put away cans and boxes.

"Still recovering. Whatever he was given packed a wallop. I heard back from one of my contacts—he thought it might have been a drug formulated to affect the metabolisms of supernatural creatures. Apparently there were a couple of witches out in the Midwest who were running a drug ring—and had connections to that dark witch Steve and Kyle helped stop up in Boone a while back."

"Drugs for supernatural creatures?" Grady questioned. "Why?"

"For all the reasons humans take them—medicine and recreation," Dawson guessed as he finished his task. "Anesthetic for a shifter or werewolf who gets hurt too badly to heal by shifting. Something to give a vampire dreamless sleep to forget the past for a while. I can see some legit reasons—and think of a bunch that aren't."

"What are you two doing today?" Denny asked.

"We're going into the shop for a few hours to make sure everything's running smoothly, and then we're taking a drive up to Cherokee. Got a call about some will-o-the-wisp lights and 'moon-eyed people' leading hikers off trails and stranding them in the woods," Dawson said. "A couple of folks fell off outcroppings, and one of them died. Not something we can ignore."

"Be careful," Denny warned. "Both the wisps and the moonies are minor fae, but they're tricky as hell. Better take plenty of salt and iron."

"Already in the trunk," Grady promised.

"You sure you're in the right head space to go after them?" Denny leveled a look at both Dawson and Grady. "They're known to influence people who are upset, and lord knows, we've had enough of that to go around lately."

"We'll be fine," Grady assured him, quickly enough that Dawson glanced at his partner, but Grady's expression looked sincere.

It should be a simple, straightforward hunt. Maybe he just needs a quick win.

Hunting was a good way to burn off anger and anxiety, and Dawson figured they'd had more than enough of both.

"We'll be back in time for dinner," Dawson assured him. "Got some stuff we need to catch you up on. Plus, don't want to miss your meatloaf."

"Damn straight," Denny agreed. "So git. Go do what you need to do and come back here. I think it would help Colt to have you around for the evening—Knox is still sleeping most of the time, and Colt can't beat me at cards."

"We'd be up for a few hands of poker after dinner," Dawson said after a glance to confirm with Grady. "See you then."

He and Grady climbed into the Mustang and left for Kingston. The morning passed quickly, and by the time he and Grady were finished at the auto body shop, Dawson had assured himself that everything essential had been delegated and covered.

They picked up a bucket of fried chicken and cans of soda from the diner and ate as Dawson drove, with the radio cranked to a classic rock station and the windows open.

"We're looking for faerie rings near where the sightings were reported," Grady reminded him. "Mushroom circles, rocks, or saplings in a perfect ring. That's the 'home base' and portal for the fae, so if we make that unusable, they'll go back where they came from—at least for a while."

"How do we do that?" Dawson had left the research up to Grady while he strengthened the protections around their house, feeling certain that they hadn't seen the last of the two extremist groups—or whoever was behind them.

"Put a handful of shiny stones in the center to call the faeries back to their base, then cover the whole ring with powdered iron and holy water," Grady replied.

"That sounds too easy," Dawson protested.

"There's one part I left out. We'll need to draw the fae out, make them reveal themselves."

"You mean, attack," Dawson countered.

"Yes, but not really," Grady hurried to reply. "They can't wander far away from their ring. If we spread the iron before we have them inside, then they're trapped out here with us. We need to know where they are so they'll be close to their ring when we put the shiny rocks in. Otherwise, they might not hurry back."

"And they aren't going to think that the two of us hanging out by their ring is suspicious?" Dawson had the feeling that he wasn't going to like the rest of the plan.

"You'll be by the ring. I'm going to draw them out."

"No." Dawson's quick, firm answer drew a frown in response.

"Hear me out," Grady argued. "Wisps and moonies are most likely to appear to people with a lot on their minds. I think the angst draws them."

"People with 'a lot on their minds'?" Dawson echoed. "What aren't you telling me?" He knew Grady had been worried and upset over Knox, and getting shot didn't help. Now he wondered if Grady had been hiding darker truths, and he'd been too distracted to notice.

"Grief," Grady said, turning his head toward the passenger window. "They are especially drawn to the bereaved and depressed, according to the lore."

"And that's you? Gray—why didn't you say something?" Dawson understood the reasons Grady might feel like that, but he felt concerned and a little hurt that Grady hadn't discussed it.

"It hasn't been going on for long, and we've had a lot of big shit going on," Grady replied, with a vulnerability in his voice that made Dawson yearn to take him in his arms and protect him.

"It's almost been a year since the hunt when Dad died," Grady spoke so quietly that Dawson turned down the radio to hear him. "And I knew the anniversary was going to be tough, but I didn't realize *how* rough." He reached out to take Dawson's hand and gave it a squeeze.

"Knox getting attacked brought up a whole lot of old hurts and disappointments that I didn't realize were still a thing," he went on. "And now, hearing Gibson and Tucker's theory about a powerful witch being involved—maybe with my grandfather and my dad, and your dad and mom—it just brought a lot of feelings to the surface."

"I'm sorry. I should have been paying more attention."

Grady shook his head. "You're not a mind reader, even if you get visions now and then. I need to use my words—only sometimes, I'm not sure how. I guess I just didn't know how to say what I was feeling. Reading Dad's journal brought back a lot of emotions. I didn't know he'd been keeping some hunts secret, and I had no idea he was looking into your parents' deaths."

"Yeah, I can see that. And tonight, we're going to have that talk with Denny whether it's a good time for it or not." Dawson sped down the straightaway, opening up the Mustang and letting her demonstrate the power of her engine.

"There's part of me that wants to know—and part that doesn't," Grady confessed. "On one hand, closure would be nice. I'd like to know for sure whether anyone was behind what happened to Dad or whether we just ran out of luck that day."

"So back to luring the fae—how is this safe if your head isn't in the right space?" Curiosity and worry twisted in Dawson's thoughts.

"I'm functioning just fine, Daw," Grady protested. "This is a way to make something good out of those feelings. One of those hikers died because the wisps led him over a cliff. The other three might have died from exposure if they hadn't been found. The kind of fae that do that choose people who feel upset and feed on the feelings."

"So you're just going to open an emotional vein in the forest and bleed until they try to lure you to your death? Because I'm really not liking this plan now that I know the details." Dawson tried to keep his voice level, but protective anger flashed through him.

"Not exactly," Grady said with a wan chuckle. "I just need to let my emotions show and stop putting up a front. They can sense pain, fear, sadness, regret—those feelings attract them. They're juicy to feed on. Once they find me, you toss the shiny stones and do the other stuff. I'm fine, the fae go home, and no more hikers get lost or killed."

Dawson wanted to argue that there had to be a different way, but he trusted Grady's research. *If Gray says this is how it works, then that's what he knows. Doesn't mean I have to like it.*

"Okay—but if I think you're in danger, I'm coming after you, and mushroom circle be damned."

"And I love you for it," Grady replied with a fond roll of his eyes. He was silent for a few minutes, and Dawson sensed that his partner was trying to think of how to phrase the next comment.

"Do you think Denny's hiding something?" Grady finally asked.

"Like what?"

"Stuff about our dads. Theories about how they *really* died. Probably to protect us—something he thinks is a good reason. But the idea that it's all linked is driving me nuts."

"Yeah, I don't think he's told us everything. And that might have kept us safe for a while—but something's changed. Now we need to lay all the cards on the table," Dawson replied. "I'm not angry with Denny. But the sheriff—that's different. Why hasn't he done more to find out who else was involved in drugging Knox? You'd think being a shifter, he'd be glad to get rid of the HDF."

"He isn't doing much to crack down on the SPS either," Grady pointed out.

Dawson shrugged. "Maybe he's doing what he can. I'm trying to give him the benefit of the doubt. I get that folks with paranormal abilities don't want to be hunted by people like the HDF scum. And humans are afraid that they're at a disadvantage against creatures with magic. But both groups are going about it all wrong."

"And as usual, the Kings are in the middle," Grady commiserated. "We don't automatically hunt everything that's supernatural or side with humans against the paranormal. So both sides think we're 'traitors.'"

"We never went into monster hunting to win popularity contests."

"True. But we also never volunteered to be targets."

"Goes with the job," Dawson said and nudged the Mustang to go a little faster until the landscape around them blurred.

The stretch of woods where the disappearances were reported lay a few miles outside the town of Cherokee. While the quaint town catered to tourists and golfers, the vast Great Smokies National Park stretched across the mountains not far beyond the city limits. Hiking trails gave visitors a taste of the forest, but large swaths of the interior were rarely visited and were home to creatures that weren't exactly human.

Dawson parked the Mustang at a trailhead and shouldered his duffel full of everything the lore said they'd need, including food, water, weapons, flares, survival gear, and a first aid kit.

"You still want to do this?" he asked Grady.

"Somebody's got to if we want to stop people from dying. Might as well be me. At least I know what I'm up against." Grady took off the amulet and removed the hex bag. "I'll take them back when we're done, but kinda defeats the purpose if the moonies can't get me, doesn't it?"

Dawson didn't like it, but he knew when Grady had made up his mind. "I've got the coordinates of where they found the 'lost' hikers and the overlook where the body was recovered. The report said the hikers started on this trail and left to follow the 'floating lights' or the 'little people.' Odds are good that the faerie ring is near there."

"It's as good a theory as any," Grady agreed. "Let's get this done."

Bright sun and a pleasant temperature for walking made Dawson wish they could just enjoy the day. Neither of them said much, although Dawson kept sneaking worried glances, and Grady was either lost in thought or pretending he didn't notice.

"That's interesting. The 'song' is different here," Grady mused.

"Yeah?"

Grady nodded. "Like a shimmer of bells." He frowned, turning in a circle to observe the other mountains. "Out there, the bells are stronger."

Dawson considered his comment. "That area is solid woods. People don't go there, no roads. Makes sense the fae would like that."

"And over there, I don't like that song at all." Grady pointed to a crest on the other side of the valley. "It's eerie. Good place to avoid."

"I always thought you were kidding when you made comments about the woods having a song," Dawson said. "Turns out you and Knox both have a little something extra."

"I never felt ashamed of mine or tried to hide it," Grady replied. "Maybe that's why it didn't mess me up. Not sure what use it has, but most of the time it makes for a nice soundtrack to a walk in the woods."

"How do you feel?" Dawson asked as they neared where the hikers had left the trail.

Grady sucked on his lip as he thought. "Pensive. I was in a pretty good mood—all things considered—when we left the parking lot. It's a beautiful day, but my thoughts keep getting darker."

"See any floating lights?"

Grady shook his head. "No. But I thought something pale and knee-height disappeared into the bushes."

"Moon-eyed people?"

"That's my guess. I could see how someone might follow to get a better look," Grady replied.

"Picking up anything new on your personal imaginary radio station?" he asked, meaning the songs of the genius loci in the mountains.

Grady gave him a look. "Actually, yes. It's like I tuned into an emo indie channel. Since you asked."

They walked for a while in silence, and Dawson figured that Grady was either listening to the mountains or falling under the spell of the fae—maybe both.

"What did the lore say about where the rings were most likely?" Dawson asked, changing the subject. The longer they walked, the more he could see Grady fidgeting, even if his partner wasn't aware of doing so.

"They're often in shady clearings near running water," Grady replied, sounding distracted. "They might be mushrooms or rocks, but they can also be swirl patterns in moss or a raised ring of taller grass in a lawn."

Grady veered closer to the edge of the path as he spoke. Dawson reached out and grabbed his arm, pulling him back to the center of the trail.

"Whoa there! Don't go wandering until we've found the circle," Dawson warned.

Grady grew quiet and more distracted, making Dawson feel sure they were getting closer to their target.

"Wait—I think I see something." Dawson grabbed Grady's hand and tugged him to follow as they left the trail and headed into a clearing.

The meadow looked like an idealized painting. Shafts of light highlighted colored leaves, and the sun shining through the trees cast the whole area in an ethereal glow. Dawson heard running water and guessed a small creek flowed nearby.

"Careful," Dawson said, making sure they didn't step into a circle by accident. Grady followed along pliantly, confirming that the fae had already whammied him.

"There!" Dawson pointed to a mushroom ring just beyond a small hillock. He pulled Grady with him and dropped their duffel next to the circle, finding it difficult to unzip the bag while also keeping Grady from wandering off.

Until they reached the circle, Grady hadn't resisted being led. Now, he started to pull away with increasing strength until he took a swing at Dawson, who let go to duck.

"Shit. They got you good, didn't they?" Dawson muttered as Grady wandered off across the meadow as if answering a pied piper's call.

Dawson grabbed the bag with the polished stones and poured them into his hand. They were the type of pretty rocks sold at tourist attractions, useful to keep on hand for spells and rituals.

Nothing in the lore said how many stones were needed to summon faeries back to their circle, so Dawson just dumped them all into the center, then he grabbed the salt and container of iron filings and waited. He kept glancing across the meadow to where Grady made his way toward the tree line, hoping his partner didn't go much farther. Dawson didn't dare leave the circle before he had completed the trap, but he dreaded having Grady out of sight.

The charged air felt like a portent of a summer storm. Dawson caught the scent of ozone, and the hair on his arms rose as the meadow fell silent. He saw what looked like a tide of fireflies streaming toward the mushroom circle from the depths of the forest. He hung back, ready with salt and iron, hoping the amulet and mojo bag protected him without calling attention to his position.

Attracted by the pretty stones, the fae didn't seem to care about anything else. A glance told Dawson that Grady had entered the woods, but he couldn't do anything about that right now.

When the last of the flickering points of light clustered inside the circle, Dawson sluiced a wave of salt across the ring, followed immediately by a flurry of iron shavings to blanket the area.

An inhuman shriek pierced the silence, and the ground under Dawson's feet trembled. He shielded his eyes as a brilliant white light shot up around the circle, extending as far into the sky as he could see.

Then the light winked out, and nothing remained except for a charred circle in the grass.

Gray. Panicked, Dawson ran in the direction Grady had gone, shouting his name. His voice echoed, but no response came.

Twigs and scrub tore at his skin and clothing. Beneath the trees it was darker, and Dawson's eyes took precious seconds to adjust.

"Grady!" he shouted, searching for footprints.

Tracking skills came in handy, and he found a partial impression of Grady's boot. Dawson set off at a jog, marveling that Grady had gone so far when he had appeared to be sleepwalking in a fae trance.

He came to a break in the underbrush, and his blood ran cold. Grady was heading for a craggy outcropping, and there was no telling how far down the drop went.

"Stop!" Dawson yelled and put on a burst of speed, tackling

Grady mere feet from the edge. They tumbled to the ground, Grady wrestling weakly, still lost in a dreamworld.

"Wake up," Dawson begged and pulled the amulet from beneath his shirt, pushing the charm into Grady's palm and closing his hand around it.

Grady went still, and he blinked rapidly. His eyes lost their glassy stare, and he relaxed in Dawson's grip.

"Daw? What happened? And why are you on top of me—not that I mind."

Dawson sighed in relief and dropped to one side, planting his ass in the moss. "They had their hooks in you, and you almost went over the ledge. I thought their hold would break when I salted the circle, but they didn't let you go on their way out."

Grady sat up and rubbed his hands over his face, still looking like he'd woken from deep sleep. "Fuck. I don't remember anything after we got out of the car."

"I figured, from the way you zoned out. It would have been funny if it hadn't been so damn scary." As it was, Dawson didn't think he'd ever feel like teasing about the situation, especially considering the drop just a few steps away.

He wondered if it was the same place the hiker had died. These mountains were full of places where primordial forces had pushed sheets of rock up from the depths and raised mountains. Boulders as big as houses and sheer drops awaited the unwary.

"I'm alright, Daw," Grady said. "You saved me—and you sent the faeries packing. That's plenty for one day."

Dawson stood and extended his hand, helping Grady to his feet. Grady glanced toward the ledge, and his eyes widened. "Damn, that *was* close."

"Let's try to avoid being bait in the future—both of us," Dawson replied.

"I'm good with that," Grady replied.

"Come on—let's go home. We've got a busy evening," Dawson said, keeping the salt and iron at hand just in case more of the fae showed up.

They both cast suspicious glances at the charred circle, but nothing interrupted their walk back to the car. Grady no longer seemed spacey, for which Dawson felt grateful, although he worried what the aftereffects of fae influence might be and resolved to see if Denny knew anything about it.

"You really don't remember anything?" Dawson had hoped that they might at least learn more about how the fae used their glamour to trap victims. He knew that ridding the forest of the faeries wasn't possible, so he wanted to be better prepared for their next encounter.

Grady frowned, thinking. "I didn't at first. Now, it's like bits of a dream. I thought I heard Dad calling to me. And then Knox—and you. You were all just ahead of me, out of sight. I wanted to find you, catch up."

He shook his head. "I wasn't scared. I knew you'd be waiting. But every time I got to where I thought I heard the voices, they were farther away, so I followed them."

"And nearly died. So we know what must have happened to the others," Dawson said grimly. He spared a glance as he drove, wanting nothing more than to take Grady into his arms and never let him go. The close call scared Dawson more than he wanted to admit. Danger might be a part of the hunting life, but now Dawson had so much more to lose than his own life.

Grady seemed to read his mind. He slipped a hand across to grip Dawson's thigh. "I'm okay. We're both safe. We won this round. You can relax."

"I don't know how to relax."

Grady licked his lips with a salacious smile. "I have some ideas."

Dawson couldn't help grinning in return. "I bet you do—and I'll take you up on them, if we're still in the mood after we have that talk with Uncle Denny."

———

"THAT MEATLOAF SMELLS GREAT," DAWSON SAID AS HE AND GRADY walked into Denny's house. His stomach rumbled, vouching for his appetite.

"How did the fae thing go?" Colt asked, busy setting the table while Denny bustled around the small kitchen, taking food out of the oven. Angel wolfed down her kibble, then wedged herself under the table.

"The stuff Grady found in the lore worked. We de-faeried that part of the woods—at least for a while," Dawson replied.

"You and Grady wash up. Colt, see if Knox is going to join us. And be quick about it—I didn't cook this just to let it get cold," Denny grumbled.

Grady and Dawson made fast work of washing hands and brushing the worst of the grass stains off their clothing. When they returned, Colt and Knox were seated at the table, and Denny motioned them toward the counter where the food was laid out like a buffet.

"Make your plates and come to the table. We want to hear all about it," Denny told them.

Grady and Dawson took turns in between bites to recount what happened in the forest. Colt and the others listened closely until they finished.

"You boys did good," Denny said. "Although it's not like we can put up signs that say 'Beware of the Fae.'"

"Maybe we should. People in these parts know the supernatural is real," Colt argued.

"Tourists don't," Knox said.

"They'll think it's a joke," Colt countered.

"Let them." Knox pushed his empty plate away. "Hike at your own risk and all that."

"Why stop there?" Denny said. "We could put up 'Vampires ahead' or 'Watch out for the werewolves,'" he added sarcastically but with a gleam of amusement in his eyes.

"Hold onto that thought," Dawson said in a wry tone. He looked to Knox. "How are you feeling?"

Knox shrugged and reached out for Colt's hand as if seeking reassurance. "Better, but not all the way yet. Whatever they gave me packed a punch."

"The downside of being human," Grady teased his brother, but Dawson could tell that Grady was relieved to see Knox up and around.

They cleaned up after dinner and took sodas with them into the living room in deference to Knox's sobriety and medication.

"You can still have beer," he said, looking chagrined. "I promise I won't jump you to drink them all."

"We don't need it. We're fine," Dawson assured Knox and looked to his uncle. "Denny—we want the real story about what happened to my parents and Uncle Aaron. Grady found Aaron's journal, and our fed friends think whoever got to them might be gunning for us next."

Knox turned wide eyes toward Dawson. "Got to them?" he repeated.

Colt looked quickly from Dawson to Denny and back to Knox. "Are you sure this is a good time—"

"Gibson and Tucker said that their supernatural forensics picked up a trace of magic with both the HDF biker boys that tried to fuck us over at the bar and those coyote shifters," Dawson continued, relentless. "They're here looking into something bigger that seems to tie in—and might have something to do with why Knox got roofied."

Dawson saw the set of Denny's jaw. "I think you've done your best to protect us all these years because knowing too much was dangerous," Dawson cajoled. "You didn't want the people who killed Grady and Knox's grandfather and my parents—and now Uncle Aaron—to get us too. But it's coming for us anyhow, and our best chance to survive is to know everything. Please, tell us."

Denny looked to Knox. "You mean what you said about not minding if I have something stronger? Because I'm gonna need it to tell this story." At Knox's nod, Denny went to the kitchen and returned with a generous portion of whiskey.

"You're sure you want to hear this? Because you can't un-hear it," he warned.

Grady gave a sad smile. "Want to? No. But we need to." He reached down to pet Angel.

Denny sat and took a gulp, closing his eyes for a few seconds. When he opened them, a resolute expression settled onto his features.

"Okay. Buckle up—this is one hell of a ride." He took a deep breath. "Frank and Rebecca Richardson—Grady's grandparents— were hunters like the Kings. They were also good friends with Michael King—Dawson's grandfather, my father."

"Frank and Rebecca were investigating a problem with rogue vampires who were kidnapping humans for food and either killing them or making them blood slaves," Denny went on. "Dangerous as hell, because it wasn't *just* vampires—Frank believed the rogues were connected somehow to vamps high up in the Syndicate. But law enforcement couldn't go after vampires, and both Frank and Rebeca apparently felt strongly about stopping the problem."

He sipped his whiskey. "I was just a kid when all this happened, so I didn't find out the details until later. All I knew at the time was that Frank and Rebecca dropped Aaron off to stay with us and the grownups talked in the kitchen for a while. Then Dad came to tell us later that Aaron's parents were dead and that he'd be living with us from now on and be adopted as a King."

"How old were you?" Grady asked.

"I was four years younger than Ethan and two years younger than Aaron. That was forty years ago, so I was six. But something like that sticks with you. Not easy to forget." Denny grimaced.

"I remember that my mom and dad argued, and then he went out. Didn't come back until almost dawn. Now that I look back on it, I think he cut a deal with one of the Syndicate vampires to leave our family alone in exchange for stopping the investigation," Denny replied. "He had three young boys, and there were plenty of other monsters to hunt. I think Dad knew he was outgunned and didn't want anyone else to die."

Denny was quiet for a moment, staring into the amber liquid in his glass like it might reveal the future. "At the time, I just remember that Mom and Dad seemed tense—probably waiting to see if we'd get attacked. Aaron was understandably a mess, having just lost both his parents, and while Ethan and I were okay with getting a new brother, we all had a lot of adjusting to do."

Denny ran a hand back through his hair. "After a while, things settled down. Dad went out on regular hunts—Mom did the research —but I guess whatever deal he made held. Time passed, we grew up, Mom and Dad retired, and then they passed away. Ethan and Aaron and I took up hunting. Plenty of monsters, but the Syndicate was never on our radar. It was just understood that they didn't kill humans, and we left them alone."

"What changed?" Knox leaned forward, caught up in the story. Angel made the rounds, moving from person to person as if she knew her presence helped to diffuse the tension.

"Not much, for a long time. Ethan got married and had Dawson, Aaron got married and had you and Grady. All the while you boys were growing up, we hunted, but they were just regular cases. Nothing huge."

He paused again, then went on. "Ethan went out on a hunt one time, and when he came back, he was real quiet, like he had a lot on his mind. He wouldn't tell Aaron or me what happened. Ethan wasn't hurt, but he wouldn't talk either. After a while, he seemed mostly back to normal, except I always thought there was something he wasn't telling us."

Denny shifted in his chair. "Then your junior year in high school, Dawson, Ethan suddenly started hunting a lot more. He and your mom went without backup from Aaron or me. I'd ask him what they were after, but he was vague. That spring, he and your mom seemed excited and nervous about something. All he'd say was that they were 'finally closing in.'"

Dawson looked down, and the loss he felt over his parents' death felt fresh and sharp. "That was right before the crash. I never did believe it was something wrong with the plane. Especially not after I found their files. You never said anything." Dawson tried to make it not sound like an accusation.

"You were grieving. I had three boys to take care of, and I'd just lost my brother and sister-in-law. We didn't hunt for a while, if you remember," Denny replied. "Or maybe you don't. You were finishing up school, Knox was having difficulty, and we didn't need trouble. I didn't want to open up a can of worms that might get someone else killed. So I locked the notes away and did my best to forget they ever existed."

"I read Dad's journal. He thought that there was a connection between what happened to his father and Ethan," Grady said. "I'd often wondered if magic could be involved."

"If you're asking whether a witch was behind the murders, I believe so," Denny replied. "Frank and Rebecca stopped the vampire who was running the kidnapping organization. A fire destroyed the rogue vamps. I think someone wanted revenge and took it by causing the explosion that killed them."

"But my parents died a long time after that," Dawson said. "More than forty years later. Aaron's death was seven years after theirs. Do you think the same witch was still involved?"

Denny shrugged. "It's not impossible—even for a human. For a vampire, even less so. You have to understand—I didn't go looking. I didn't talk about it with Ethan or Aaron. If they tried to bring up what happened, I wouldn't answer. The Kings are the guardians of this mountain, but we don't have to sacrifice everyone we love to it."

Denny looked away and took a slug of the whiskey. Dawson felt missing pieces slot together in his mind as he looked at his uncle. *Denny never married. Did he lose someone to monsters—or to hunting? Or did he not try to find a partner, worried they wouldn't be safe? He took me in after my parents died. After Aaron was killed, he took Grady in and looked out for Knox. And all this while, was he hiding the secret of what killed his brothers?*

"Dad and I were attacked by a werewolf," Grady said. "Was it more than what it seemed?"

Denny turned back to them, and Dawson saw raw emotion in his uncle's eyes. "I don't know. I honestly don't. I wish I did. At first, I wanted to believe it was just a bad hunt. Then later, I wondered if someone had sent that werewolf to finish the job and get you and Aaron out of the way."

He shook his head. "I'm sorry. I thought that steering clear would keep you safe. Now I wonder if I'd helped Ethan instead of stonewalling him would it have not only saved his life but Aaron's as well."

"You did the best you could," Grady told Denny. "It made sense to stop investigating. You couldn't have known they'd still come after us."

"Where does the attack on Knox come in?" Colt asked. "Is it really as simple as him overhearing something in the bar? Or was someone going to come after him sooner or later?"

"What I saw in Dad's journal made me think that Knox was safe because he quit hunting after his accident," Grady said, with a quick glance toward his brother, who looked away.

"I hope that's the case. But I think that maybe it's time to look at the files I have from Frank and Ethan—and some of Aaron's that weren't with your other stuff," Denny said with a nod toward Grady, "and see if we can get to the bottom of this. Having backup from those feds wouldn't hurt."

"You'd trust the feds?" Dawson asked. "Because I don't completely trust Sheriff Rollins—just putting my cards on the table."

"Rollins is a hard guy to like sometimes," Denny replied. "I can't blame him for being pissed about that 'prank' Ethan and Aaron played. That was way over the line. They shouldn't have done that. And I don't think they would have if they'd realized that Rollins would hold a grudge this long."

"Rollins and most of his deputies are shifters," Dawson said. "Do you think they're sympathizers with the Supernatural Protection Front?"

Denny frowned. "Beau Rollins? I don't think so. Rollins takes himself and his job too seriously sometimes, but his respect for the law is what's at the bottom of most of the run-ins he's had with the

Kings over the years. So breaking his oath to support a terrorist group? He's not my favorite person, but I really don't see that in him."

"What about other members of the sheriff's department?" Grady pressed. "They're shifters—if one or more of them liked the SPS, would Rollins even find out?"

"Rollins has good instincts, or he wouldn't have lasted this long," Denny replied. "I don't think he'd put up with that kind of thing—if he knew. Could someone lie to him? Probably, but not forever."

"How do you want to play this with Gibson and Tucker?" Dawson asked. "I think they could be allies, especially if the case they're investigating is tied in with the deaths in our family. But then again, we don't *really* know them, and I don't want to accidentally confess to too much illegal stuff in front of federal agents."

Denny finished off his whiskey in one slug. "Good question. Here's what I think we ought to do. Accept their help and find out what they know. At the same time, we go through the files and journals that Frank, Ethan, and Aaron left behind and see whether we think that their reasoning made sense. Wouldn't be the first time a hunter saw a conspiracy where there was just a run of bad luck and poor choices. Then if we think there's a solid case to be made for the witch angle, and if the feds are going down a similar track, we share what's relevant. Sound good?"

They all nodded. Denny got up and walked his glass out to the kitchen. "Better get a good night's sleep, boys," he said when he returned. "Because we've got a shit ton of files to go through in the morning."

Denny left them and headed to bed. Dawson wondered if it was a ruse so that he didn't have to answer more questions or talk about a subject that clearly still brought back the grief of losing so many loved ones.

Everyone else needed time to let the disturbing information settle. Colt and Knox slid to one side of the big couch while Grady and Dawson took the other end, and they streamed a favorite action flick. Wrung dry by Denny's revelations, they actually watched the familiar movie instead of making out with their partners. Angel snuffled in her sleep and rolled onto her back with all four paws in the air.

When the credits rolled, Colt and Knox stood. Dawson noticed that Knox seemed a bit unsteady. Colt wrapped an arm around Knox's waist immediately, stabilizing him and saving his dignity.

"That was one hell of an after-dinner conversation." Colt tried to sound nonchalant and managed to just sound exhausted. "I'm beat, and Knox is supposed to get plenty of sleep, so we're going to call it a night."

"Yeah, I guess we should too," Dawson agreed. "Early morning, long day from what Denny said. But if we don't have a hunt, Grady and I need to spend the morning at the auto body shop. I appreciate people covering for us, but I don't want anyone to feel taken advantage of."

"I've already spoken to the assistant manager at the hardware," Colt said. "Knox is on medical leave for as long as it takes." Colt's job as a programmer enabled him to work from home, giving him the flexibility to look after Knox. The two shuffled down the hallway, and Dawson heard their door click shut. Angel followed, nosing open the door to Denny's room.

"Come on," he said, wrapping an arm around Grady. "Let's get some shut-eye."

They got cleaned up for bed and slipped beneath the covers. Grady rolled toward Dawson and snuggled into his side. Dawson brought his arm up over Grady's shoulders and tangled their legs together.

"Tell me what you want," he murmured and kissed the top of Grady's head.

"This. I need to be all wrapped up in you, feel you, breathe your scent. I'm too stressed out for anything else, but I want to feel safe," Grady whispered.

Dawson's heart broke for the vulnerability he heard in Grady's voice, and he gathered him closer, angling their bodies so he knew Grady could hear his heartbeat. "I'm here for you—however you need me," he promised, tracing slow circles on Grady's back like he was soothing a child roused from nightmares.

Grady made a satisfied snuffle and wriggled even closer. Dawson held him tight, trying not to relive his terror over Grady's near miss in the forest and his panic at seeing the fae-glazed look in his lover's eyes.

He could have died. He might have survived but lost his mind and self to the moon people. My parents loved each other, and their time together was cut short. They had the chance to show the world how much they loved each other and make it official. I want that with Grady so badly.

Should I ask him soon, despite everything crazy that's going on? Our lives are never normal, but right now things are insane even for us. Maybe it's not a good time for a life-changing question.

But what if something happens to one of us? What if I wait for a better time and lose the chance completely?

Grady's even breathing told Dawson his partner had fallen asleep. He knew he would be sore in the morning from the awkward angle of his arm. The warmth of Grady's body was already raising a sheen of sweat despite the cool night, but Dawson didn't want to break contact or move apart.

I've got to protect Grady first, or the rest doesn't matter. But once this nightmare is over, I'm going to make sure the whole world knows that he's mine.

6

GRADY

"I'm surprised that so many ghosts have stuck around here after all these years," Grady said as he and Dawson walked the grounds of the long-defunct Cragmont Sanitarium.

"Maybe they're afraid to move on. Or maybe they were here long enough it's home." Dawson carried a shovel and a duffel bag, and Grady had a shotgun with rock salt rounds in case any of the Cragmont's "guests" decided to get rowdy.

"It's just so sad that they came here to get well and never were able to go home," Grady mused.

The Cragmont sat on the ridge of a hill, a large four-story wooden building with a gabled roof and wide porches circling the three main floors. Back in the early 1900s, tuberculosis patients came to these mountains hoping that the clean, cold air would ease the damage to their lungs. Before antibiotics, the incurable disease eventually claimed its victims, many of whom died in their twenties.

The annual trek to make sure the ghosts of Cragmont stayed in their resting place always made Grady pensive. The big building looked more like a grand lodge than a hospital and must have had beautiful views when the surrounding area remained largely unsettled.

"How long have you been coming out here to walk the pipes?" Grady asked as Dawson used a metal detector to follow the iron pipes filled with salt that had been buried around the entire perimeter of the old building to keep its ghosts inside.

"Since high school," Dawson replied, intent on the pings from the detector that let him know he was following the right trail. "I started coming out here with Dad, then later...after...with Uncle Denny."

"Did they tell you who buried the pipes? It's a smart idea, although with a building this big, it must have taken a long time." Salt and iron dispelled ghosts, so the pipe was a barrier the spirits couldn't cross.

"I've heard a couple of versions. The sanatorium closed back in the 1940s, so several people have gotten credit for the idea. I think it was Grandpa Michael's father who actually created it. I'm grateful. I'd rather not deal with the ghosts one-on-one."

Grady knew that eventually salt would eat through the iron. Maybe they'd pushed their luck already and were on borrowed time before the ghosts broke loose.

"Did you ever go inside?" He looked across the weeds toward the shuttered hospital. Despite long disuse, most of the windows were still unbroken, and the old building remained in surprisingly good shape. The porch roof sagged in places, and the paint peeled from the siding. Grady wondered whether the floor was solid enough to hold his weight and what the ghosts did all alone in such a place.

"Once. Colt and I were supposed to check to see if there'd been a break in the pipe—we'd gotten reports of ghost sightings, and this seemed like the logical place to start. We were young, cocky, and fearless. We jumped the pipe and decided to explore."

Dawson gave a rueful chuckle. "We were stupid. But it certainly was exciting. Nearly got our asses handed to us by the ghosts."

"Really?"

"There must be hundreds of them—people who died here and didn't move on. Some of them are sad, others are angry, and some have just faded to nearly nothing," Dawson went on, turning to look at the hospital. "I don't know what they would have done if they had caught us. We fought our way clear. I've never crossed the pipe since then."

"I think they heard you." Grady looked past Dawson toward the building and saw a line of gray figures watching them from the other side of the salt and iron.

The ghosts stood silently, hollow-eyed and sullen, wearing shapeless shifts that might have been dressing gowns. As quickly as they appeared, they blinked in and out, always in different places, hurling themselves against the invisible barrier the salt and iron created.

"They're looking for a weak spot," Dawson said as Grady stumbled backward. "When they were alive, they wanted to leave. That might be the only thing they still remember—needing to get out."

"Can't someone say a blessing—or an exorcism?" Grady felt torn between pity and fear.

"We send out a priest every year," Dawson said. "Denny handles that part."

He pointed toward where the ghosts tested the line most often. "Let's bury extra salt and iron there—the spirits sense a weakness. These weren't dangerous people when they were alive, but a century of wandering hasn't helped them. I don't trust that they won't hurt us —even if they might not mean to."

Grady held the shotgun ready, covering Dawson as he dug into the dirt. The ghosts surged again, just as Dawson's shovel clanged against something metal.

"Dammit—the pipe's rusted through—"

The temperature dropped, and half a dozen spirits slipped across the barrier. They hurled Dawson out of the way before he could spread salt to stop them. Grady pulled the trigger, sending a blast of rock salt through the closest ghost and into the narrow breach in the warding.

The next moment, invisible hands shoved him out of the way to land hard on the ground. The gray figure of an angry woman loomed over him, letting out a terrible shriek as her hands reached for his throat.

"Stay down!" Dawson warned, swinging the shovel through the hazy form that had Grady pinned.

The ghost winked out, and Grady rolled to his feet, firing past Dawson's shoulder as two more spirits closed on them.

"Go!" Grady told Dawson when the revenants vanished in the hail of salt. "Fix the hole. I'll cover you."

Dawson tried to get close to the broken pipe and scattered a line of salt to keep out more spirits. But every time he started to dig, spectral hands reached through the gap, trying to grab and claw.

Before he could talk himself out of it, Grady jumped across the pipe into the dead zone, standing in front of the gap with his shotgun raised. "I've got this—block the hole."

He didn't dare look back, but he could picture Dawson's thunderous scowl. Dawson sloshed salt around Grady's feet to give him a safe place to stand and then went back to rapid digging.

More ghosts gathered, watching Grady. Most looked curious, but an aura of malice surrounded some of the spirits.

"Stay back," he warned them, reminding himself that for him, freedom was a step backward across the pipe barrier.

A rock flew through the air, aimed at Grady's head. He ducked—and one foot moved outside the sparsely-salted ground. Hands clutched him and pulled him off balance shoving him so that he stumbled. The shotgun was ripped from his hands and tossed aside. He tried to dodge back to where he'd been, only to be pushed again, away from the pipe circle and closer to the old hospital.

"Gray!" Dawson shouted, working frantically to patch the hole in the salt pipe so the rest of the ghosts didn't escape.

"Dig faster!" Grady shouted as the ghosts buffeted him across the short expanse of overgrown lawn. Another ghost rammed into him, and he nearly fell. They were herding him toward the dilapidated building, and Grady had no desire to see the inside for himself.

The ghosts are shoving me, but they aren't grabbing and holding. He wracked his brain for why things had changed because he'd been choked and pinned by ghosts more times than he wanted to remember. *Maybe the amulet or the mojo bag repel their touch.*

"Fuck this." Dawson laid the salt-filled pipe in the shallow trench and poured a thick layer of salt on the ground just behind it, double-sealing the gap. "I'm coming!"

He jumped over the barrier and picked up the fallen shotgun, sending a blast to Grady's right into the gray cloud of spirits clustered all around.

"They can't stand to touch and hold on," Grady yelled as the ghosts knocked him from one side and the other. "I think it's the charms." A ghostly fist to the stomach doubled him over. The air around him felt like a meat locker, making him cold enough to shiver and raising goosebumps on his arms.

Dawson fired again, and the press of spirits dispersed. He jogged up to Grady and grabbed him by the hand. As soon as their skin touched, Grady felt a jolt that he saw mirrored in Dawson's flinch. The ghosts drew back immediately, leaving them surrounded but with several feet between them and the spirits.

"I don't know what's in those protective charms, but it's working," Dawson said, keeping hold of Grady's hand.

"Let's edge our way back toward the pipe circle," Grady suggested. "We might have to make a break for it at the end, but if you've put a Band-aid on the pipe, we can get back without them following."

"Do it," Dawson said, keeping hold of Grady with his left hand and the shotgun with his right.

They moved a step at a time, and the combined juju of the talismans they wore kept the ghosts about three feet away. When they finally crossed the lawn, that left them a yard away from the edge of the circle, with a half dozen ghosts between them and freedom.

"Ready?" Dawson asked with a devil-may-care smile Grady knew hid his fear.

"Born ready," Grady snarked.

Dawson loosed another two shotgun blasts in quick succession, blowing away the ghosts who blocked them. They dove over the pipe, pursued by the other spirits which were brought up short when they hit the newly-reinforced invisible barrier.

"You okay?" Dawson asked, giving Grady a careful once-over.

"Yeah, you?"

Dawson nodded. "I didn't get thrown around as much as you did."

Grady dusted himself off, looking ruefully at grass stains that were unlikely to come out of his jeans. "The first ghost went for my throat but didn't touch me. Something about the amulet kept them back, so they shoved and bumped but couldn't grab."

"That energy when I touched your hand was really weird," Dawson admitted. "But the result was like 'Wonder Twin powers, activate!'"

Grady looked at him, horrified. "Please don't ever say that again."

Dawson reached out and took Grady's hand. "I don't feel that strange surge."

"Neither do I."

"Maybe it just works when we're in danger, and the amulet and mojo bag are working," Dawson suggested. "As grateful as I am for the protection—and as much as it probably saved both of us an ass-kicking right now, I'd like to know more about how they work and what they do. I don't want to guess wrong and get fucked over."

When Dawson finished reinforcing the weak spot, he covered the new pipe with dirt and sprinkled more salt on it. "This needs a more permanent fix where the pipe is rusted through. I'll tell Denny, and he'll get it taken care of when he sends the priest."

They were quiet for a while as they walked back to the Mustang, still jangled and alert from the ghosts' attack.

Finally, Grady spoke. "The ghosts made me remember something I've been wondering for a while. Do you think what they say is true about the souls of the Kings coming back to the mountain, protecting us? And would that count for Dad and Grandpa Frank? Because they weren't really Kings by blood," he continued. "Sometimes, I think that adopting Dad brought bad luck to the family."

Dawson stopped and turned to face Grady. He set his hands on Grady's shoulders and looked him in the eye. "You are the best thing that ever happened to me. I will never believe that anything about what brought us together was bad luck."

Grady felt Dawson's grip tighten. "You and Aaron and Knox are

Kings of the heart," Dawson went on, "which is all that matters. As for spirits returning here, Denny says it's not true. Been a rumor for probably as long as the Kings have been in these hills. Maybe some ghosts choose to come back, but the spirit of these mountains is something much, much older—it was here long before we came, and it'll be here long after we're gone. And if it decides to lend a hand now and again—or sing to you—I'll take all the help I can get."

He smiled at Grady and leaned in to kiss him. "Besides, I don't need the ghosts of my ancestors looking out for me. I've got you and Denny."

Grady cast a backward glance at the Cragmont, but the ghosts were gone, and all that remained was a ramshackle building. He shuddered and gripped Dawson's hand tighter.

"With everything that's been going on, have you gotten any visions? It would be kinda nice to get some cheat codes on how to deal with all the crap that's been going on."

Dawson sighed. "Nothing useful—just snippets. Didn't mention them because I didn't want to worry anyone. Maybe something else will give me enough context for the visions to be useful."

"Tell me."

Dawson shrugged. "I saw a cabin in the woods—no idea where. Nothing special about it. A white SUV in an intersection. No license plate. Like I said—snippets. And since having a vision isn't fun, it would be nice to get a dream that unlocks the next level," he added, staying with the video game metaphor Grady used.

"I've never thought I had any extra abilities—unless you count hearing mountains sing," Grady replied, deciding to bring up something that had been bothering him for a while. "But all the time we were growing up, Knox had a freaky way of knowing things sometimes that he shouldn't have known. Dad used to yell at him for spying on people or going through their things, but I don't think that was true. He just *knew*."

"Some kind of psychic talent?" Dawson replied, holding Grady's hand as they walked the last stretch of driveway toward the car.

"I guess that's what you'd call it. Not exactly premonitions like your dreams, but just having information pop into his head that turned out to be true—that he shouldn't have had any way of knowing," Grady replied. "Dad didn't want to deal with it, so Knox stopped asking questions. But I've always wondered...if he had some natural talent, and it got pushed down and ignored, could that have led to some of the other problems?"

Dawson let out a low whistle. "You mean like Knox was using the stuff he took to self-medicate? Make the ability go away?"

Grady nodded. "Yeah."

Dawson shrugged. "I don't know much about that sort of thing, but they say whatever you bottle up comes to the surface eventually." He paused and frowned as if remembering something. "Back when I was hunting with Knox, before his accident, he used to have this weird ability to find things that were lost or hidden. I chalked it up to luck. But now I wonder—and I think you might be right."

"Kings hunt monsters," Grady replied as they reached the car. "We know the supernatural is real, but when it comes to magic or psychic abilities, people get skittish." He shook his head. "Like Gibson and Tucker—a witch and a psychic. My dad would have been antsy about that. Not that he wouldn't have accepted the help, but he wouldn't have been completely comfortable with it."

"And you think Knox picked up on that, so he hid what he could do?" Dawson asked as he turned the key and the Mustang's engine revved to life.

"I think it's possible. And if that's what he did, then it was stupid. Magic or abilities are tools—like being good at math or having a gift for music. This is a dangerous business—having a little something extra on our side sure wouldn't hurt." Grady rubbed a hand over his ribs, unconsciously soothing the scars of the werewolf fight that claimed his father and nearly got him too.

"Maybe it's time to have a conversation with Knox and let him know we're okay with any abilities he wants to tell us about," Dawson suggested. "Now that he's sober, those 'insights' might start coming more often. I want to make sure he knows that he doesn't have to hide."

They drove home instead of to Denny's place, needing some downtime before they had to be around people. Dawson called Denny to let them know they were safe and gave him a short recap with the promise of a more in-depth recounting when they came for dinner that night.

Sharing a shower gave Grady the chance to check his lover thoroughly for injuries, and Dawson returned the favor. As Grady had predicted, he'd have some bruises, but nothing serious. He knew they were both lucky and didn't want to think about what might have happened without the amulets—or if the ghosts had succeeded in dragging him into the old hospital.

"Earth to Grady?" Dawson murmured and ran a soap-slick hand up and down Grady's half-hard cock for emphasis.

"Hmm?"

"Oh, that got your attention," Dawson said with a chuckle, shifting so that his stiff dick rode the cleft in Grady's ass.

"Always. And the answer is yes."

"Where did your brain wander when my hand was on your prick?"

"Probably wondering when you're going to deliver what you're promising," Grady replied, pulling himself out of his thoughts and trying not to darken the mood.

Despite great pressure and a nearly endless hot water supply, shower sex didn't last long. Dawson rutted between Grady's ass cheeks while he reached around to get Grady off. The water sluiced away the evidence, leaving them warm, clean, and relaxed.

"I wish we could just go to bed and stay there," Grady murmured once they were dry and dressed. "We've earned it."

"Yeah, me too," Dawson agreed. "But Denny hates being stood up when he's expecting us—can't blame him—and I'm sure whatever he's making is better than what I'm motivated to cook."

"And we owe him a report and our suspicions about the amulets," Grady supplied.

Dawson's phone rang, and he glanced at the name. "Gibson," he told Grady before he answered the call, putting it on speaker.

"We've got something new," Gibson told him. "Are you available?"

"Diner?" Dawson suggested.

"Not the kind of stuff we should discuss in public," Gibson replied. "Your place or our cabin?"

Dawson shot a look at Grady. "We can be at your place in fifteen minutes. That okay? We've got dinner plans."

Grady tried not to snicker. Dawson made it sound fancy. Denny would be flattered.

"Can do. We've got coffee and donuts. Investigations don't happen without them," Gibson joked. "Better hurry or Tucker will eat all the good ones."

"Thanks for the warning. See you then." Dawson sighed. "So much for downtime. You ready to go?"

"As ready as I'm going to be. At least we'll have the feds' news to report to Denny as well as ours," Grady replied, hoping that the agents had made progress.

Gibson met them at the door. "Come in. Donuts are on the table, and we just made a new pot of coffee."

Grady chose a raspberry filled donut, while Dawson picked a maple frosted. They settled in at the small table, and the other men took seats across from them.

"Supernatural forensics confirm that the trace magic on the HDF bikers' corpses is the same power signature as on the coyote shifters' bodies—and the bar brawlers from The Maverick," Gibson said as Tucker reached for another donut.

"And that supports your witch theory?" Grady asked.

"It's not confirmation, but it's a step in that direction," Gibson replied.

"How much do the Kings get involved with the Syndicate?" Tucker asked, with powdered sugar dusting his russet beard.

"We don't," Dawson replied. "Unless supernatural creatures kill people or traffic other cryptids, we leave the rest to the human authorities. We're monster hunters, not law enforcement."

"Do you think your fathers and Grady's grandfather knew that the cases that got them killed involved a Syndicate rogue vampire and his pet witch?" Gibson took a drink of his coffee and waited.

"We're not sure what they knew," Dawson replied. "We think my dad and Grady's grandpa were chasing blood slave traffickers. If the vampires had Syndicate ties, that wasn't where the concern lay. As for the witch—there's a good chance he or she is the one behind the deaths."

Grady was quiet for a moment. "I agree with Daw. Stopping the rogue vampire was the goal. They wouldn't have seen it as going up against the Syndicate. Those groups have rules about interacting with humans. Usually when someone breaks the rules in a big way, the pack or nest leaves them to the hunters."

"And *usually* you'd be right," Tucker said. "Except that the rogue vamp your grandfather went after was the blood son of a powerful elder in the Syndicate. And whether by design or not, your grandparents burned the vamp—which the elder took as a war crime, worse than just killing him. Even if he did recognize that his son had crossed too many lines for the behavior to be ignored."

Grady paled, and Dawson put a steadying hand on his arm. "My grandparents burned to death," he said. "The insurance company and the police said it was arson—regular human-style. But apparently magic was involved?"

"We think Ophelia Locklear was the witch helping the rogue vamp," Gibson said. "Not entirely clear on their relationship, but it's likely that either she was injured in the fire that killed Frank Richardson and his wife, or Ophelia took her vampire partner's death personally and lashed out for revenge."

"That doesn't explain what happened decades later to my parents," Dawson said, tightening his grip on Grady's arm, anchoring them both.

Gibson sat back and stretched his long legs out to the side. "My suspicion? Ethan had no idea at first that the case he and your mom were chasing was connected to Frank's death. Somewhere along the line, they figured out that the cases overlapped, and that probably pushed them to take more risks for the sake of vengeance."

"If Ophelia found another partner for some new scheme and Ethan started nosing around, she would immediately think the Kings were on to her—again," Tucker added. "She either didn't bother protecting her partner or wasn't able to—but she saved herself and caused your parents' plane to malfunction as revenge."

"And then *my* dad stumbled upon his father's files and started digging," Grady said with a sigh. "But we were hunting a werewolf when he died. That case had nothing to do with vampires or the Syndicate or witches."

"We got a DNA match on the blood of the werewolf that killed your father—and tried to kill you," Gibson replied. "He wasn't just an out-of-control were. Taren Villers was a hitman who happened to be a werewolf. The hunt was a setup. You were both supposed to die."

Grady felt like he might throw up. *A hitman. We walked into a trap.*

"Gray?" Dawson asked quietly, concern clear in his voice.

Grady managed a nod. "Let me guess—Villars was connected to Ophelia."

Gibson and Tucker both nodded. "Yeah," Tucker confirmed. "She might have caught wind of yet another King digging up the past and decided to nip the problem in the bud."

"Except we killed the hitman," Grady said with a note of pride in his voice. "You're saying that you think the witch sent the hitman? Why would she kill my grandparents and Dawson's parents herself but outsource us?" He couldn't completely hide the way he flinched at the words.

"Our theory is that she's been weakened somehow, and that's why she hired a killer," Gibson replied. "She's still dangerous—just not as powerful as before."

"And since you killed the hitman, she's going to be out for revenge —again," Dawson warned.

"I still don't understand her endgame," Grady said. "Why would the past matter so much now? And if she's really involved with the SPS like you thought, what's in it for her?"

"We're still trying to figure that out," Gibson admitted. "We showed up because it looked like someone with Syndicate ties was starting up the blood trafficking again. We even had a come-to-Jesus-meeting, so to speak, with the head of the vampire side of the business. And it surprises the shit out of me to say this, but I think he was telling the truth. What's going on, isn't the Syndicate's fault."

"The vampires aren't involved with whoever is using the legend of the Bushwhacker 'ghosts' to kill people. In fact, they'd like to find Ophelia themselves—apparently, she double-crossed them," Tucker added.

"And the Bushwhackers? Do you think that's Ophelia? Because both HDF and SPS supporters have turned up dead," Grady asked.

"Still figuring that out," Gibson said. "We haven't found more bodies—but we also haven't found the last five people they took aside from the bikers. None of the missing people had ties to either of the extremist groups. They were just hikers or tourists who disappeared. No one's heard from them, and at this point, they're presumed dead."

"It's more than five," Tucker said. "Those are just the ones who were reported missing in the nearby towns. When we broadened the search for people who disappeared while traveling in Western North Carolina, we found twenty unresolved disappearances in the last two years."

"Twenty?" Grady echoed.

"Afraid so," Gibson answered. "We're still looking into it. This has all the markings of a supernatural case—we're just not sure how it all goes together. We aren't finished—just wanted to give you an update and warn you to watch your back. Ophelia's still out there—and she's got a grudge against your family."

Grady's phone alarm reminded them it was time to leave for dinner. They promised to stay in touch with the two agents and headed for Denny's house.

"What did you think of that?" Dawson asked as he drove away.

Grady closed his eyes and sagged against the seat. "I'm glad Gibson and Tucker are working the information from their end, but it feels like we're all missing the point somehow. Twenty missing people —presumed dead—who aren't HDF or SPS. So the bodies found were purposely left to send a message—but was it a warning or a threat? The feds came looking for trafficking, but that doesn't seem to be going on. So why were those hikers taken and killed? And does it have to do with Ophelia—or us?"

"I don't know," Dawson admitted. "But I don't like how it seems to revolve around our family."

"I think we need to tell Denny everything. Kings are good at figuring things out. We just have to put our minds to it," Grady said with more optimism than he felt, for Dawson's sake.

———

DENNY AND ANGEL GREETED THEM AT THE DOOR, AND GRADY WAS pleased to see that Knox was out of bed, sitting in the living room with Colt. He looked a little too thin, and he had dark circles under his eyes, but he was upright and smiling at Colt, so Grady took that as a hopeful sign.

Conversation stayed light through dinner which included a hearty pot roast with carrots and potatoes, freshly baked bread, and apple pie for dessert. They talked about TV shows and movies, local gossip, and funny memories—everything except hunting. Angel wriggled under the table, forcing them all to shift their feet. Grady couldn't help feeling like it was the calm before the storm.

After dinner, Dawson and Grady laid out everything they had learned, as well as their suspicions and the update from the agents.

"We need to see all the files," Dawson told Denny. "If Gibson and Tucker are right, this witch took our families—and she's coming after us next."

Grady turned to look Knox in the eye. "I need the truth. You *know* things that you have no way of knowing. And you always have."

Knox didn't say anything, and Colt took his hand. Finally, Knox nodded. "Yes. For a long while, I didn't understand. I just thought I was weird. When I tried to tell people, it didn't go well. Dad was afraid—never knew whether it was *for* me or *of* me. So I just quit talking about it and tried to pretend it didn't exist."

"But that didn't work, either," Grady supplied. "And eventually, it caused problems."

Knox nodded. "Yeah. Looking back, I should have known that would happen, but I was just a kid. When Mom left, I thought it was because I wasn't normal."

"That wasn't—" Grady started, but Knox cut him off.

"I realize she left for her own reasons—now. But I was hurt and angry, and her leaving messed up you and Dad a lot, and that just made me even more sure that I needed to bury the weird stuff deep." He sighed. "It didn't work, of course. So I tried to knock myself out."

"He's clairvoyant," Colt said with a hint of defiance in his voice. "Your cousin Max knows some people at this psychic place in New York, and they helped Knox figure out his talent."

Knox looked like he might argue, but Colt silenced him with a look. "It's a *talent*. An *ability*. Not a curse or a burden." Colt looked back at them, shifting to put himself slightly in front of Knox. "Part of getting sober means learning to accept that part of himself. Don't fuck this up for him."

"I told Aaron he was making a mistake," Denny spoke up. Everyone looked at him. "He was a mess when your mother left—and I'll never forgive Camille for what she did to all of you because she couldn't stand hunting. But Aaron had his own issues."

Denny got up and poured a slug of whiskey into his coffee, standing at the counter with his back to them for so long Grady didn't know if the older man was going to finish his story. Finally, Denny brought his cup back to the table.

"No one ever treated Aaron any different because he was adopted. But in Aaron's mind, he had to prove he was 'good enough' to be a King. Not just as good as everyone else—better. I think that, to him, anything 'unusual' meant not fitting in."

"But I've had visions since I was a kid," Dawson countered. "No one made a big deal out of it."

Denny shrugged. "You were a King by blood. You and your father didn't have anything to prove. Neither did Aaron—but no one could ever convince him of that."

So everything Knox has gone through was because Dad had an inferiority complex? I loved him, and I miss him, but right now, I'd like to take a swing at him for the damage he caused, Grady thought. *Good thing I never mentioned hearing mountains sing.*

"The people Max connected me with are teaching me how to use what I can do," Knox said hesitantly as if he was still expecting rejection. "We've just gotten started, so don't expect miracles. But someday, maybe my clairvoyance can help with hunts even though I can't go out in the field anymore." He rubbed absently at his bum leg.

"You don't have to earn your place," Dawson reassured. "I'm sorry if anyone made you feel like that. Even if you never use your talent, it's okay. The hardware store is important to the community. You don't have to hunt. Just—accept what you can do, and don't worry what anyone else thinks."

The relief on Knox's face made Grady's heart break a little. Colt still looked defiant and protective, and Grady loved him for watching out for Knox. *I'm glad Colt accepts him for who he is—in all ways—but Knox should have felt that from the rest of us all this time.*

"I never thought much about what happened to Grady's Grandpa Frank until Ethan and Jackie got killed," Denny confessed. "Then I found all the research Ethan had done and the files that belonged to Frank. I hid them, figuring nothing good could come of it. I didn't realize that Aaron had started digging into the past until after he died, and I found his notes—everything except for the journal."

"Ignoring what they learned didn't keep us safe. So if you want to pick up where they left off, I won't stand in your way," Denny went on. "Hell, I'll help any way I can."

Denny set his cup in the sink and went to the storage room while Grady and the others cleared the table. Angel seemed to realize the food was gone and padded into the living room. When Denny returned, he was carrying two large boxes.

"This is everything—except for that journal you held onto," he said with a nod to Grady. "There's a lot here, so everyone take a stack, and we can work through it. I brought some tablets and pens for taking notes—you can bring your computers tomorrow if you'd rather. Here's my thought—Colt and Knox, take Aaron's notes. Dawson and Grady, go through Ethan's. I'll work on what Frank left us. We're not going to read everything tonight, but we can at least get a feel for what's here."

Colt and Knox took their pile of papers into the living room. Denny took one side of the kitchen table while Grady and Dawson took the other.

For a long while, no one said much as each group inventoried their part of the information. Grady poured over the pages in front of him. He bumped shoulders now and again with Dawson when he could tell that his partner was becoming overwhelmed by the emotion of sorting through his father's notes.

"I know what it feels like," Grady told him quietly. "That night you found me reading Dad's journal—in my mind, I read every word in his voice."

Grady didn't expect that they'd get much further than just organizing the piles in front of them, and he was correct. After a couple of hours, all of them were yawning and bleary-eyed. Despite the urgency, he knew that pulling an all-nighter would do more harm than good. Angel had collected pats and ear scratches from everyone and stretched out on the floor, snoring quietly.

"I'm going to call it a night—for all of us," Denny said just after midnight. "Might as well get some shut-eye and start again tomorrow. Don't want to miss something important because we were falling asleep."

The others reluctantly agreed. Grady felt glad for the break since he could see that the files were taking a toll on Dawson's mood.

"Come on," Grady said. "Denny's right. We'll get a fresh start in the morning, and you'll feel better. I'll even help make French toast for breakfast," he added with a grin.

They said good night and traipsed off to the room they always shared at Denny's. Once the door shut behind them, Dawson pulled Grady into a kiss.

"Thanks for watching out for me. Seeing all that in Dad's hand-writing—it brought back a lot of feelings," Dawson explained.

"I'd offer to take your mind off things, but after the day we've had, I'm honestly beat. Let's set an alarm and catch some sleep—and if we wake up horny and do something about it, that's a bonus."

"I like the way you think," Dawson teased, but he didn't argue as Grady headed to the queen-sized bed and climbed under the covers. Grady dutifully set the alarm on his phone so that they stood a chance of waking up at a decent hour.

Grady realized how quickly he'd fallen asleep when he heard Dawson mumbling under his breath as his body began to buck and jerk.

Shit. It's a vision.

"Daw? C'mon Daw—wake up. You're safe. We're home. Whatever you're seeing—it can't hurt you."

"No...stop...don't..." Dawson's fitfulness continued as if he hadn't heard anything Grady said.

By now, Grady had grown used to Dawson's visions, but they never ceased to make him wonder and worry. He didn't know how Dawson received the information from his dreams—and neither did Dawson—but he was never wrong, although a lack of details and context might make the reality different from the appearance.

"Daw—please. I need you here with me. Wake up and we'll handle it together," Grady cajoled.

Dawson's body lost its tension, and his features relaxed, shedding their stress. His eyes blinked open, and his gaze darted frantically around the darkened room before he saw Grady.

"You're home. We're safe," Grady soothed. "Breathe."

Dawson shook his head. "Not safe. Fire. Need to warn Denny and Knox."

"Someone's going to set fire to Denny's house?"

"No. The hardware store. Someone's going to try to burn it down."

7

DAWSON

"What the hell, Dawson? Where the fuck are you two going at three in the goddamn morning?" Denny, grouchier than usual after being awakened, glared at them through bleary eyes. Angel sat next to him, looking displeased at having her sleep disturbed.

"Gotta stop a fire." Dawson and Grady had pulled on clothing so fast in the dark that only now did he realize they had switched their shirts.

"You're not making any sense, boy. Slow down."

"Had a vision. Someone's going to burn the hardware shop. Need to stop them," Dawson explained as he laced his boots.

"The sheriff—" Denny objected.

"Isn't going to believe me." Dawson cut him off. "We haven't exactly spread it around that I see things that haven't happened yet. Can't imagine he'd be willing to get someone out of bed without evidence."

"What's going on?" Colt and Knox came to the kitchen doorway looking rumpled.

"Dawson says he's had a warning about a fire," Denny remarked.

Knox's eyes widened, and he paled. "Fuck. He's right. I didn't know it before, but now that he's said it, I'm sure." He looked to

Dawson. "There are delivery pallets in the alley behind the store. Go there first."

"I'm coming with you." Colt looked defiant.

"We've wasted enough time. Stay here, and make sure someone doesn't try to torch the house," Dawson snapped. "I doubt this is a one-man arson."

He grabbed Grady's arm and maneuvered them both out the door. "Stay inside and keep your eyes open," he called over his shoulder to the others. "I'll call when it's over."

As they got into the car, Dawson tossed his phone to Grady. "Call Gibson. I don't care if it's three-o-fuck-in the morning. Tell him what's going on. Sheriff Rollins won't move his ass for this, but I'm betting Tucker and Gibson will."

The Mustang roared into the night. Dawson had a white-knuckled grip on the steering wheel as Grady made the call and put the phone on speaker. Gibson answered on the second ring.

"King—what's up?" He sounded far too alert, and Dawson suspected the agent hadn't yet gone to sleep.

"This is Grady. Dawson had a vision about arson at Knox's hardware store. We're heading there. Can you back us up?"

"Visions? No one said anything about fucking visions. Now?"

"Yeah," Grady snapped. "Do you have our backs or not?"

"Don't get your panties in a wad. We'll meet you there."

A weather alert sounded on Dawson's phone. Grady glanced at the screen. "Storms coming in. High winds, thunder, heavy rain. Dark and stormy night, huh?"

"Just our luck."

Grady ended the call and sat stiffly in the passenger seat, tension having obliterated any remnants of sleep. "What, exactly, did you see?" Grady asked as they raced down the darkened road.

"A shadowy figure slinking around outside the store, and then the whole place going up in flames," Dawson replied, voice tight. "Been having these visions long enough that I know the feel of one that's a 'maybe' or a 'soon' and a 'right the hell now.' This was *now*."

"Watch out!" Grady shouted as a huge buck with flaming antlers appeared from nowhere to block the road.

"Hold on!" Dawson had no room to maneuver. He braced for impact, with no choice except to hit the creature head-on.

The Mustang raced right through the figure, which vanished around it like smoke, although it had looked solid seconds before.

Dawson's stomach clenched and his heart pounded. "You okay?" he managed, breathless.

Grady nodded, taking a moment to find words. "Was that a—?"

"A not-deer," Dawson replied, taking a deep breath to still the way his body shook from adrenaline.

"There was something wrong with the way its eyes were on its head," Grady began.

Dawson spared him a glance. "There was something wrong with the *flaming antlers!*"

From the split-second glimpse he'd gotten, Dawson knew that Grady was right. "It looked like a computer graphic of a deer's face—if the artist had never seen a real one."

"Shit. Isn't it bad luck to see a not-deer?" Grady asked.

"Only people who are in danger are supposed to be able to see them. Well, there's a surprise."

Dawson's fingers drummed against the steering wheel as the muscle car hugged the tight curves of the mountain road, flattening the hills with its speed. The engine's purr was a growl tonight, and Dawson found himself spoiling for a fight.

The Mustang was fast but not quiet. Dawson parked her a block away, pausing just long enough to grab their weapons before they sprinted toward Kingston Hardware.

Streetlights and store security lighting didn't reveal any suspicious figures, but Dawson knew that didn't mean the danger had been averted. He and Grady advanced, guns in hand.

Dawson could feel the coming storm with the way the wind had kicked up.

Knox's hardware store took up most of its block, with an alley running behind it. Dawson signaled for Grady to go right, crossing in front of the shop and down the other side, while Dawson went along the left.

There. Dawson spotted movement near the wooden pallets as Knox had predicted. He ran toward the hunched figure in a black hoodie as the smell of gasoline confirmed his worst fears.

If I shot at him, would a spark set off the gas? With the wind, a fire could take out the whole block.

Dawson ran and dove, tackling the arsonist from behind and taking them both to the ground, but not before the man tossed a lighter into the pile. The dry pallets went up in flames with a *whoosh* as he wrestled with the man and tried to pin him to the ground.

Hoodie Man slammed a fist into Dawson's temple, tearing free and tossing Dawson close enough to the flaming pallets that embers burned his skin, and fire licked at his boots. The man ran down the alley, and Dawson climbed to his feet to give chase.

Two shots rang out. *Grady.*

Flames leapt high into the darkness against the brick back wall of the store. Dawson pulled his phone out and dialed 911 as he ran toward where he'd heard the gunfire.

"Fire at Kingston Hardware. Arson. Hurry." He ended the call and shoved the phone back in his pocket.

"Daw!" Grady shouted. "Over here!"

Dawson made out a standing silhouette and something crouched on the ground. He slowed and advanced cautiously, gun raised.

"You okay?" Dawson called to his partner, keeping his Taurus leveled at Hoodie Man, who lay on the street, clutching his leg.

"I'm fine. He's got a bullet in his knee," Grady replied. "Sucks to be him."

A movement in the shadows made Dawson pivot, gun trained on the darkness. "Come out real slow," he ordered.

"You called us, remember?" Gibson stepped into the light. "Looks like you didn't need the backup after all."

"We had no idea what we were walking into. Thanks for coming. Where's your buddy?" Dawson tried to look around Gibson into the night.

"Down there," Gibson replied with a jerk of his head to indicate the fire. "Wanted to get a look before the forensics were completely fucked all to hell."

Gibson turned to eye the scene. "Could have been a lot worse. I checked around front—no explosives, no long fuses. Looks like this guy wanted to stay in the dark—like a roach."

Sirens sounded, echoing from the walls of the buildings around them. Emergency flashers and bright headlights lit up the alley as a fire truck and ambulance arrived, and the fire crew swung into action to save the hardware store and the buildings around it.

A sheriff's vehicle blocked the other end of the alley. "Guns on the ground, hands in the air," a voice sounded over a bullhorn.

Dawson and Grady moved slowly to comply, warily watching their captive. Gibson responded with jazz hands and a "don't fuck with me" expression.

"I've got a shiv in my boot," Dawson growled to the arsonist. "I can be on you in a heartbeat, so don't try anything."

"Dawson and Grady King—why am I not surprised?" Sheriff Rollins barked as he walked into the alley, backed by two deputies. "And a fed. What the fuck is going on?"

Dawson glanced over his shoulder and saw that the firefighters were soaking the pallets to contain the blaze. He sighed in relief that the fire had done minimal damage and hadn't spread.

"Got a tip that someone was going to try to burn down the hardware store," Dawson told the pissed-off sheriff. He reminded himself that it was close to four in the morning, and everyone had been dragged out of bed. "Came over to keep that from happening and found this scumbag lighting the pallets."

"So you shot him?" the sheriff thundered.

"He was fleeing the scene of a crime, and he charged me. I was afraid for my life," Grady replied, deadpan.

"Bet if you check his priors, he's either Human Defense Front or Supernatural Protection Society," Dawson challenged. "He seemed to know his way around starting a gasoline fire."

Rollins pinched the bridge of his nose like he was fighting off a headache. He turned his flashlight beam on the downed man. "You got something to say for yourself?"

"Bunch of fuckin' hunters," the arsonist shot back. "Better 'freak' than weak."

Dawson recognized the slogan as one of the SPS phrases. "Except that silver bullet put a crimp in your style now, didn't it?"

"Need a medic!" Rollins bellowed to the firefighters at the other end of the street, and a soot-streaked man soon jogged up carrying an emergency kit. He knelt to examine the injured arsonist's knee while the sheriff kept his weapon trained on the prisoner.

"Try to keep him from bleeding out until we get him to a hospital and into a cell," Rollins growled.

"Better make sure he's got a guard on his door all night and he's cuffed to the bed with silver," Gibson said. "We'll take custody in the morning."

"Oh, we'll make sure he doesn't go anywhere," Rollins promised. "But about the custody—not until I've processed him for what he's done. You can have his carcass when I'm through."

The sheriff turned to Dawson and Grady. "Don't think this is over. I'm going to want statements from both of you. Especially about that 'tip' you got. So don't leave town."

An ambulance pulled up, lights flashing. Rollins and his deputy stood watch as the crew got the injured arsonist onto a gurney and into the back of the vehicle, then the deputy followed in the SUV.

Dawson and Grady picked up their guns and tucked them into their waistbands. "Thanks for showing up," Dawson said as Tucker strode up to join them.

"We were still awake," Tucker replied. Something in his voice suggested that it was work, not sex, that had kept them up.

"New leads?" Grady asked.

Gibson glanced around them. "Nothing solid yet. Research pays off...but it's a bitch until then."

Wind howled down the alley, stirring up ashes and sending embers into the air as the firefighters hosed down the hot spots and adjacent buildings.

Dawson called Denny. "We got here in time—but it was close. No telling if this guy acted alone." He glanced at Grady. "We're going to go check our house. Better keep the lights on and make sure Angel is on guard duty."

"Will do," Denny said. "Colt and Knox—and Angel—can hold the fort here—I'll go check the main auto shop location."

"Don't take these assholes on by yourself," Dawson cautioned.

"I'm not stupid," Denny replied in a dry tone. "Kinda thought I'd just run anyone over with my truck if I see something. Go check the house, and come back here when you're ready. Be careful."

"You too." Dawson ended the call.

"Why don't we tail you while you make sure everything's okay," Gibson suggested, and Dawson accepted the backup with gratitude.

To his relief, they found no evidence of tampering around their house. Colt and Denny called to confirm that their patrols had not turned up new dangers. For the first time since his vision, Dawson relaxed.

"Let's get breakfast," Tucker suggested. "There's a Waffle House not far from here. Unless the storm is going to be one for the record books, it'll be open."

Gibson chuckled. "The Waffle House Index?"

"It's never wrong," Grady replied.

The all-night diner chain was famous for remaining open through all kinds of weather. On the very rare occasions when a catastrophe forced locations to close, it was regarded as an omen. Even the National Weather Service respected the Waffle House Index.

Fifteen minutes later, they sat in a back booth under the relentlessly bright fluorescent lights that were as much of a trademark as the chain's glaring yellow signage.

"This is a heart attack on a plate," Gibson said, shaking his head as he looked at the menu.

"And it's worth every bite," Tucker replied enthusiastically.

"I call it a reward for a hunt gone right." Grady looked up as the server came and ordered coffee for all of them. "I'm not going to worry about cholesterol when there are rougarous out there."

Grady ordered smothered hash browns with bacon, while Dawson had his usual pecan waffles. Tucker grinned like it was Christmas as he ordered steak and eggs, and Gibson had two eggs over easy with buttered toast.

"Life is short," Tucker said with a mouthful of steak as he stole a slice of bacon from Gibson's plate. "Never pass up bacon."

"You'll have to excuse him," Gibson said with a fond sigh. "He gets sentimental over pork products."

Dawson suspected that his ravenous hunger came from the same place as the horniness that often followed a hunt. *Proof of life.* It didn't matter that he could still smell the gasoline and taste it in the back of his throat, or that he'd be blowing ash-tainted snot from his nose for days. Right here, right now, they were alive, and they'd saved Knox's store—and a chunk of downtown Kingston.

That made it a good night.

"We're going to run that guy's data through our systems," Gibson said, dropping his voice. "Not that I don't trust your local cops, but—"

"He doesn't," Tucker finished for him. "Might be wrong, but a little paranoia is good for the lifespan."

"Unlike bacon," Gibson returned.

"Bite me."

Gibson sighed. "Can't take him anywhere."

Outside, the storm had picked up, driving the rain against the diner's large windowpane-walls and whistling across the roof.

"No need to hurry eating—unless you want to drown on the way to the car," Grady said. "At least there's no chance of the fire re-igniting."

Dawson sipped his coffee. "Why do you think they went after the hardware store instead of the auto body shop? Seems like a strange choice."

Gibson sat back in the booth and cradled his cup in his hands. "Not if the grudge comes down through his grandfather and father." He leveled his gaze at Grady. "Which means you need to keep your guard up. Maybe you're thinking about this all wrong."

"What do you mean?" Dawson asked, worried.

"You're looking at it as a vendetta against the Kings. Maybe it's really a grudge against the Richardsons," Gibson replied.

Grady caught his breath. Dawson slipped his hand beneath the table to twine their fingers together in support.

"But my parents were killed too. And they weren't Richardsons," Dawson challenged. Even as he spoke, he guessed the answer.

Dad and Mom picked up on Frank Richardson's case. They got too close, and that sealed their fate. So it was the Richardson connection.

Grady pushed his food away, half-eaten.

Tucker gave him a look. "Not hungry? You barely ate?"

"Still a little nauseous from the smoke, I guess."

Dawson knew Grady was lying, and he had a good idea why. That topic would have to wait until they were alone. He turned back to the two agents.

"Now what? The asshole who tried to burn the store talked like SPS. They don't like us much because we side with the humans when someone with abilities goes too far," Dawson said. "Are you going to take the guy into federal custody?"

"Probably not, but I want a crack at questioning him," Gibson replied. "Ophelia's covered her tracks well, but someone, somewhere, knows something—and we'll find it, eventually."

The sun still hadn't risen by the time they finished their food and paid the bill. The rain eased to a drizzle, but dark clouds suggested a downpour could happen again at any minute. Dawson had seen the predictions, and the weather for the next few days would be lousy. Gibson drove them back to where Dawson had left the Mustang parked. The cops and fire trucks were long gone, but the smell of smoke still hung in the air despite the rain.

"Stay in touch," Gibson told them. "And keep your eyes open. The guy tonight didn't act alone. We'll keep working on our end. Let us know if you think you've found anything."

Grady was quiet on the drive to Denny's house. Now that the adrenaline had crashed and breakfast settled in his gut, Dawson was ready for a shower and a long nap. But he knew that before those could happen, he needed to clear the air with Grady.

"I know what you're thinking," Dawson said quietly.

"Oh, really?" Grady sounded sad, not angry, which made Dawson's heart ache even more.

"What Gibson said about the Richardson angle, it's—"

"True." Grady turned to look at him. "Grandpa Frank started this war. And if Grandpa Michael hadn't adopted Dad, the witch's vendetta against Frank wouldn't have gotten tangled up with the Kings. It's our fault."

Dawson veered into the parking lot of a darkened store and stopped the car. His expression silenced Grady's questioning look. "None of this is your fault, or Uncle Aaron's, or Grandpa Frank's. They did what they were raised to do—hunt creatures who use their abilities to hurt people. And sometimes, those creatures fight back."

"This vendetta killed your parents," Grady protested, sounding miserable.

"My parents were hunters," Dawson countered. "They knew the risks. Dad considered Aaron to be his brother just as much as he did Denny. I'm certain he and Mom started looking into Frank's notes because they stumbled across the connection and then because he worried about harm coming to Aaron—and you and Knox."

"But—"

"No 'but.' Even if another family had taken in Aaron when Grandpa Frank died, what's to say one of the King brothers wouldn't have gotten involved somewhere down the line?" He shook his head. "Please, Grady—don't take this on yourself. I don't blame you, and Denny doesn't either. And I promise you, we're going to find that Ophelia bitch and end this."

Grady looked hopeful and heartbroken. Dawson leaned over to kiss him, careful not to move fast enough to make his seatbelt catch. Grady kissed him back, more reassuring than heated.

"Come on. Let's go back to Denny's and go to bed. We can fill everyone else in after we've gotten some shuteye."

8

GRADY

"Wake up, sleepyheads. It's already noon." Denny's voice accompanied several loud raps on the door to the room Grady shared with Dawson. Angel barked, adding emphasis.

Grady groaned and poked Dawson in the ribs. "Do we gotta?"

"Why doesn't sleeping four a.m. to noon feel the same as midnight to eight?" Dawson grumbled.

Denny hammered on the door again. "Lunch is going to get cold. I'm not heating it up for you. And the sheriff wants your asses down at the station to give statements."

"We gotta." Dawson sighed. "Fuck."

They had showered to get the stink of the fire out of their hair and the ash off their skin before collapsing and thrown their smoky clothes in the laundry room. That meant it only required getting dressed and a quick turn through the bathroom before they stumbled to the kitchen.

"I feel hungover, and I didn't drink anything but coffee," Dawson muttered.

"We're getting old," Grady commiserated.

"Oh, quit whining," Denny said, overhearing the comment. "I've got T-shirts older than either of you."

He pointed a spatula toward an iron skillet filled with hash brown casserole. "Eat."

Grady paused long enough to draw the curtain back and look outside. "Ugh. Looks like those predictions about the storms are holding true. Those black clouds look like trouble."

"They're coming in faster and harder than the Weather Service said," Knox commented as he passed Grady on the way to the table. The certainty in his voice suggested this was an insight from his ability, not just an observation.

"Good to know." *How long did we all just brush off Knox's "opinions" instead of realizing that he had a gift? No wonder the guy had issues.*

Denny gave the table over to the four younger men and leaned against the counter as he ate. Angel lay at his feet but kept an eye out for any dropped food.

"I'm going to double-check the wardings on Aaron's house—yours and Dawson's now—and this one, and on Colt and Knox's apartment," Denny announced. "I still think that until we get this shit resolved, Colt and Knox are safest here. Can't do as much to protect rented property."

Grady knew Colt and Knox had grown closer over the past few months and spent nearly all their time together. He hadn't heard that they had formally moved in together and gave his brother the stink eye.

"I was going to tell you," Knox said with a shrug. "Not like it's a secret. It just didn't come up."

"His lease was done at the end of last month, and my place is newer and has more room," Colt said, patting Knox's hand and giving Grady a smile to smooth things over. "So it's very new. Not like he wasn't staying over most nights anyhow."

Did Knox think I'd disapprove or not believe he was recovered enough to make a decision like that? Or have I been so wrapped up with hunting and rebuilding what Daw and I have that I wasn't paying attention? Knox is my brother. I need to do better. I'll make it up to him, Grady promised himself.

"We're going in to the hardware store," Knox said, raising his head as if expecting pushback. "I need to talk to the staff and see the damage. I'd like to hire a security guard—we just have to make sure they're not HDF or SPS."

"I'm going with him," Colt said. "We won't take any chances—I swear."

"Not going to argue with any of that," Dawson said. "We're heading to the auto body shop in Kingston to make sure the staff are okay. I'm planning to hire security as well—we'll get Gibson and Tucker to vet them. I'll snag one more for you."

"Thanks," Knox replied, and his pleased look of surprise broke Grady's heart a little.

———

SPENDING THE DAY AT THE SHOP CLEARED GRADY'S HEAD. THEY WERE as candid as possible with the employees, all of whom knew about the King's "other" business. Dawson didn't go into more detail than necessary, only that the fire at the hardware store was case-related and a vendetta against the family.

When he put it up to a vote whether to stay open with added security or close for the rest of the week, the staff all voted to keep the shop working. Grady saw how overwhelmed Dawson was with their trust and gave his hand a reassuring squeeze.

By evening they had a short list of security candidates for round-the-clock-shifts at both the main auto shop and the hardware store, starting immediately, that were cleared through Gibson by the TBSI. Thanks to Colt, they also had security cameras installed at the two businesses, and after some debate, at their houses as well.

"It's not bulletproof, but having guards and cameras is a damn sight better than not having them," Dawson said once the security officer was in place. "I wish it were as simple protecting the houses."

Grady understood. Since the Kings were already well-armed and seasoned monster hunters, anything coming against them at their homes was likely to be fueled by magic, not muscle.

"Denny's upping the protections. And if we can figure out this case, maybe all the extra precautions won't be necessary for long," Grady replied, trying to be hopeful.

Dawson leaned back in his office chair. "Fuck, I hope so. Our cases don't usually disrupt business, which screws things over for everyone else. I want to stop Ophelia and get back to normal."

"Doubt it's going to be quite that easy, but I'm ready to be done with this case as well," Grady agreed.

Outside, dark skies and high winds gave the evening an ominous feel that Grady couldn't shake. Dawson had bought pizza for the whole crew, an additional "thank you" for their support, and the workday ended on an upbeat note. Now that everyone was gone for the day except him, Dawson, and the new guard, Grady felt uncomfortable and exposed.

"What's on your mind?" Denny asked, jostling Grady's shoulder.

"Everything," Grady admitted. "The storm's got me jittery."

"Let's see what Gibson and Tucker have learned from their sources and what Denny's hunter contacts have come back with. We might find exactly what we need to crack this case wide open and get rid of old Ophelia once and for all."

"I wish we were married," Grady blurted, saying aloud what had been on his mind all day. "I know we can't right now, but with what we do—it feels like tempting fate to put it off. We're it for each other, always have been. I guess I'm just scared that something might happen before we get the chance."

Dawson pulled him into his arms. "Hunting's dangerous. But we're not reckless. We've got allies. We're taking precautions. I haven't had any new visions—I'd tell you if I did."

I'm afraid one of us will get killed protecting the other. I'm afraid the witch will find a way to keep us apart. I'm afraid that now that I've finally got the thing I wanted most, something might take this away from us. Grady didn't know how to put any of that into words, so he just leaned into Dawson and trusted the other man to read his body language.

"Hey," Dawson said, tilting Grady's face up so that their eyes met.

"We're going to fight this witch and win. Settle the score. And we're both going to walk away from it—together. I believe in us."

Grady managed a smile. "I believe too. It's just that this time, the attacks are personal."

"And we'll make sure the payback is too," Dawson vowed. "Don't let the fear get to your head. We've got this."

Chaz, the new night guard, came on duty, and Dawson double-checked him against the information Gibson had vetted.

"I'll check all the doors once an hour and keep my eyes on the exterior security cams," Chaz promised. "I'll take good care of the place."

They went out the front door, and Chaz locked up behind them. A crack of thunder and lightning flash shook the world, and rain came down in bucketfuls, drenching them before they'd gone two feet toward where the Mustang was parked.

Dawson lengthened his stride to get out of the rain, and Grady hurried behind him. That put Dawson a couple of yards ahead, crossing the street when the traffic light changed as a white SUV pulled up, blocking Grady's path and his view.

The SUV's back door flew open, and Grady saw a woman dressed in gray inside. She spoke strange words, and Grady found himself unable to move. Rough hands pulled him inside the vehicle, and he tumbled to the floor as the SUV roared away.

Grady heard Dawson shout and then the sound of gunshots. *Daw —be safe.*

"Got him," a man's voice said from the front seat. "He won't be chasing us."

Daw? Grady's heart sank, and he struggled harder against invisible bonds, alert and aware but helpless. The SUV rumbled down streets, taking corners at high speed, throwing Grady around the floor. He rammed the newly stitched wound on his arm and swallowed back a cry of pain.

"Don't fight," the woman told him. "You can't break the spell. No one's coming for you. There's a distraction spell on this vehicle that makes it nearly impossible to trace. By the time they know you're gone, you'll be somewhere they can't reach."

Ophelia Locklear. The witch kidnapped me, I can't move, and Daw's been shot, maybe killed. Fuck. This is bad, very bad.

Grady tried to remember the turns the driver took, but there were too many switchbacks and too long a ride. He recalled what his father had taught him about getting out of ropes and zip ties. *Relax. Exhale. See if that gives me a little slack.*

That might have been good advice for normal bindings, but the magic stayed wrapped tightly around him. He tried to calm his mind so he could think clearly. *If I can't use my body, then I have to use my mind. It's the only weapon I can control right now.*

Grady breathed deep until he mastered the panic. First, he focused on the sounds and scents inside the SUV. Ophelia smelled of herbs and incense, and her bracelets jangled when she moved. From the driver, Grady caught the smell of cigarettes and the smack of chewing gum. He couldn't get a good look at the shooter in the passenger seat, but he did pick up the reek of cheap cologne.

The SUV wasn't remarkable, standard issue without visible upgrades. From the hum of the road, Grady knew they were still on well-paved routes, so they hadn't turned onto the smaller, private roads that were often dirt or gravel.

Then he heard the song. Faint at first, the sound grew clearer, and Grady strained to listen. He had spent years of his life in these mountains and had grown to recognize the "signature" music he associated with specific places. Some were faint and hardly memorable. Others took his breath away with their beauty no matter how often he heard them. A few haunted his nightmares, bad places he knew to avoid.

He recognized the song that grew stronger as the SUV drove on. *It's the bad mountain from when Daw and I stopped the fae. Why the fuck are we going closer? Daw will never think to look for me there.*

Daw might not be able to look for me. Those gunshots—

Grady had to stop and take more deep breaths to calm himself. *I've got to keep it together. That's the only way I'm going to make it home.*

Since breaking loose didn't appear to be an option at the moment,

Grady tried to get a feel for the power that bound him, anything to keep from panicking over Dawson and the shots he'd heard.

Ophelia's magic tingled like a light electric charge running up and down his body. When he struggled, the tingle grew stronger around the pressure points, becoming more and more uncomfortable.

The amulet and mojo bag don't seem to be helping. Or would it be worse without them? If she doesn't notice, are they something I can use to get free?

I've got to get back to Dawson.

Grady refused to believe Ophelia's taunts or the shooter's comment. *They want to fuck with my mind. Daw's okay. He has to be okay.*

After a long drive, the SUV stopped. By now, the discordant, ominous song of the mountain's spirit nearly overwhelmed him, stoking despair. Although the ethereal music had not grown louder, it seemed more intense. Grady strained to pick up details, like the toll of funeral bells instead of the glissando of chimes.

But why is it like that? What makes the difference? And if this is a bad place with a malicious natural spirit, why did Ophelia choose to be here?

"Get him inside," the witch ordered. Grady went limp, protesting in the only way he could.

"Fuck, he weighs a ton," the driver said as he and the man in the passenger seat—*the one who shot Daw*—lifted Grady by his feet and shoulders and carried him along a forest path.

A sturdy cabin sat at the end of the trail, hidden by trees. Grady had no landmarks, but he felt sure this was the fake Bushwhackers' hideout, the one that had eluded their previous search. *If we didn't find it before, how will anyone find me now?*

No one is coming to save me. I'm going to have to save myself.

The goons dropped him unceremoniously on the floor in the cabin's small living room. Grady landed face up and got his first good look at the witch who had torn his family apart for three generations.

"Grady King. I've had my eye on you." Ophelia Locklear looked to be in her early fifties, but Grady knew she had to be much older. For as much damage as she had caused, Grady expected to confront the living embodiment of a Disney villain.

Instead, he found himself facing a woman who wouldn't have been out of place or remarkable at a bake sale or the public library. Ophelia's gray-flecked dark hair flattered very average features in a short, modern cut. She wasn't willowy like movie sorceresses. He guessed her to be about five and a half feet tall, a bit plump, dressed in boots, jeans, and a long-sleeved gray T-shirt.

Destructive magic wrapped in a commonplace disguise, all the more dangerous because it was so easy to overlook.

Since the binding spell kept him from speaking, Grady glared at her, picturing in detail the bloody retribution he wanted to exact.

"You resemble your grandfather," she said, eyeing him like a piece of art. "Take after your father too. Guess that brother of yours looks like your mother. She was the only smart one in the lot—took off for the hills when she realized what hunters were really like."

She turned toward him so that he saw her full face and not merely her profile. Ophelia had scars that ran from her left temple to her chin, puckered like burns. Long sleeves hid her arms, but her left hand also bore pink scars.

Was she injured when she killed my grandfather or Daw's parents? He didn't begrudge himself a flare of pride that his family had exacted a toll on their killer, even in death.

I've got to keep my wits about me and figure out what she wants. If she intended to kill me, she could have done it already. She's keeping me alive— for now. There's got to be a reason.

His blood ran cold. *Am I bait to draw the others? Even if Daw is... hurt...the guard saw enough to know there's trouble. Denny and Gibson and Knox will come looking.*

You're a hunter. You're trained for this. Act like it! Grady berated himself. He took one deep breath and then another, letting calmness cool the incandescent fury inside.

"Maybe I'll let you speak—let you ask all the questions burning up in that little hunter mind of yours," Ophelia mused. "It's not like you'll be telling anyone. In case you were wondering—I am going to kill you. Just not right away."

She gave him a head-to-toe lingering glance that made his skin crawl. "You're young and strong. You'll last a while. So much energy and anger. So...potent." The smile she gave him felt like fingernails scraping his bones.

Shit. She's describing me like a battery. Is that why she's not a mummy by now? Maybe she didn't just hijack the Bushwhacker ghost legends on this cycle—maybe she's been behind it for a long time.

Thinking about the witch kept Grady from obsessing about Dawson or spiraling over how screwed he was.

Think! If I can figure this out and get free, we can set this whole bloody "family curse" thing to rest.

Self-doubt flooded in immediately. *If Grandpa Michael and Uncle Ethan and Dad couldn't beat her, why do I think I can? I don't exactly have an advantage here.*

Or maybe I do. Did the others have a chance to observe her, or did they only meet in a fight? Maybe if I watch closely, I'll find a weakness. I've got to believe I can do something to make this right.

The witch looked at Grady with contempt. "Your family nearly cost me my magic. All because they would not die easy." She bit off each of the last four words. "The first two put up quite a fight. It took a lot to destroy them—but I did. Burned them like they did my patron, my mentor."

Ophelia's calm delivery made her words all the more chilling for the lack of emotion. "The next two hunters cost me my lover. Killing them destroyed the fire drake I'd summoned and bound—and almost tore my magic out by the roots." Her smile reminded Grady of a corpse's lips drawn in by death over its teeth. Her smile emphasized the burn scars on her face.

"I had time while I recovered to plan my revenge. Since the Richardsons and Kings like to hunt, I figured I'd lead them on a merry chase, give them a mystery to solve, and kill the rest of them one at a time." Ophelia's expression changed from confident to vindictive, then verging on crazed. Grady couldn't do more than glare.

"Move him out of the way so we don't trip over him. Chain him in the corner." She waved her hand, and the spell that kept Grady immobilized vanished.

145

The driver dragged Grady to the corner and cut the zip ties that bound him, holding him still while the shooter fastened steel cuffs around his wrists that were attached to solid chains bolted to the wall.

Guess I'm not the first "houseguest" they've had.

"You get a bucket for your needs and food when we eat. Give us trouble, and you go without," the shooter warned.

"Your fake 'Bushwhackers' killed those coyote shifters—and the bikers," Grady accused, figuring that if he died here, he'd at least have answers.

Ophelia turned to look at him, perhaps surprised that he was defiant enough to question her. "Of course. The ghosts were a convenient fiction. The coyote shifters weren't from a local pack. They were drifters. And the bikers were enemies, thinking that humans without powers should be protected."

Grady wondered if the driver and shooter were Supernatural Protection Society. He figured it likely. *What's to keep her from quietly backing both the HDF and the SPS from behind the scenes and making sure they both have enough grievances that they stay stirred up? That creates a nice smoke screen for whatever Ophelia herself causes.*

He wondered how loyal his captors would be if they knew Ophelia might be playing the SPS off against the HDF—with herself as the only winner.

I'll keep that to myself for now. Can't prove it, and they won't believe me. But maybe I can get her monologuing. Keeps her from doing worse.

"A fire drake? That's hefty magic." If Ophelia was telling the truth, Grady was grudgingly impressed. He thought the stories of being able to summon and control such creatures—small fire-breathing lizards—were just folktales.

"I bound it to me, and the drake made quick work of your grandfather—and your uncle," she gloated. "But the damnable creature broke loose during that last fight, and I killed it when I couldn't bind it again. A costly victory." Bitterness colored her voice.

"So you came here to hide and lick your wounds?" Grady knew that annoying Ophelia might get him killed, but he had a chance to find out what really lay behind the tragedies that had damaged his family, which pushed him into dangerous territory.

"Is that why you had to hire a hitman to kill my dad and me? Weren't up to it yourself?" Grady couldn't help the accusation, voicing the question that had tormented him since he had learned the truth.

"Unlike the Kings, I don't have the spirits of my dead family returning to the mountains to give me strength," she spat. "I took the energy of the ones I kidnapped. I will never be weak again."

"Lady, I don't know who told you that dead Kings are the spirits of Cunanoon Mountain, but they lied. Those genius loci were here long before the Kings, and they'll be here when the land sinks back under the sea. If tapping that is your end game, it's not going to happen."

"You're wrong!" Ophelia's voice rose to a shriek. "Liar! That's why the Kings are so hard to kill. Once I break that link, they'll be as easy to destroy as everyone else."

"We're just good at what we do. We make our own luck," Grady told her, daring to meet her gaze. "How did you think you were going to cut the family off from the spirits of the hills? Wave your hand? Light a candle?"

"Open the mounds and release the dark fae and their creatures," Ophelia replied, eyes glinting with madness. "They will obey me, and those of us with magic will take our rightful place ruling over those without."

The crazy is strong with this one, Grady thought. *No wonder the SPS goons love her. They've missed the part where she's the queen and they're the drones.*

Cold dread shivered through him at her words. *Open the mounds? Release the dark fae? She's fucking mad. They'll destroy all of us—and she'll be first in line.*

"The mound fae have been imprisoned for millennia. How are you going to do that?" Grady feared that if Ophelia ended the rant, he would never get the answers he craved.

A cruel smile twisted Ophelia's features, something that Grady thought belonged to a serial killer—maybe an apt comparison.

"You'll see. I'll have a guest shortly who will be very interested to meet you."

With that, Ophelia turned and walked away, leaving Grady to his unanswered questions.

Once the witch and her two goons went to the kitchen to eat, Grady tested the chain and his cuffs. *Standard steel, no sigils or magic. Solid and heavy, but mundane.*

Now that he could move, he slowly shifted his hand to find the amulet that still hung beneath his shirt. As soon as he clasped it in his palm, he felt better, as if it cleansed the last of Ophelia's spell from him.

Grady found a way to raise a pinprick of blood on his finger from a sharp edge on the cuff's hinge and pressed the crimson droplet to the mojo bag that had gone unnoticed in his pocket. If feeding the *entity* in the bag tightened its bond with him, Grady was open to all the help he could get.

Ophelia's so certain that she has the upper hand she never even searched my pockets. My gun's gone, but my wallet's still in my back pocket. Tonight, when they sleep, I'll get the lock pick that's in my wallet. Maybe I can get out of these cuffs. If I can run into the forest, the song of the mountains will guide me home.

The driver brought him a bucket and turned his back while Grady fumbled with his fly to relieve himself.

"If you take a shit, I'm making you slop the bucket out into the john," the man warned. He took the bucket, walked into the hallway, and moments later, Grady heard a toilet flush.

At least I didn't have to piss myself. A little dignity left before she kills me.

Grady ate the sandwich the shooter brought him, cheese slices on dry bread and a can of generic lukewarm soda. He hated the thought of taking food from the hand of the man who had shot Dawson, but Grady knew he needed to keep his strength up if he was going to escape—or fight to the last.

The sound of bells made him look up sharply. This wasn't the tinkle of chimes like Grady had heard at the fairy ring. The heavy, ominous clang reminded him of a death knell.

"Daelin. Welcome." Ophelia's entire manner changed. Her honeyed tone was in glaring opposition to the screech she had directed at Grady moments earlier. Even her appearance was different, and Grady guessed it was a trick of her magic.

"My lady, you are gracious."

The newcomer might have been the most elegant being Grady had ever seen; tall, slim, and with an other-worldly, ethereal beauty that told him this must be one of the fae.

A heartbeat later, and Grady's vision glitched like a bad video. Superimposed over the beauty was a hideous face, gaunt like an old corpse, all sharp angles. This was the fae's natural appearance, its beauty nothing but a glamour.

One monster helping another.

"Is the ritual arranged? I don't want to wait," Ophelia sounded imperious, like a queen to a commoner. Grady had the distinct impression that Daelin had the upper hand.

Why does that name sound familiar? Grady had always been fascinated by stories of the fae, although he never expected to meet one— had fervently hoped not to, given their tricky and sometimes blood-thirsty reputation.

Not Daelin. The Dullahan. The horseman. Reaper of souls. This is not good. Not good at all.

"Tomorrow night is auspicious," Daelin told her. "All will be as we have planned."

He turned, seeming to notice Grady for the first time. Grady shied away from the cold gaze and caught a glimpse of sharp teeth behind blood-red lips.

"This one has a bit of a shine to him," Daelin remarked. "He will feed you well and give you power for the ritual."

"The last time that's needed," Ophelia said, looking at Grady as if eyeing a meal. "Once the mound is opened, that won't be necessary anymore."

"You are correct, my lady," Daelin said. "After that happens, you won't need to borrow power ever again."

Ophelia seemed to take the fae's words as a promise. Grady read the ominous intent immediately. *You won't need to borrow because you'll already be dead,* he thought. *Not like I'm going to warn her. She wouldn't believe me anyhow.*

The witch and the fae left the room, talking quietly, and stepped outside, leaving the two goons in the cabin's small kitchen. Grady slumped against the wall, devastated at this new twist.

Opening the mound and letting the dark fae loose will kill everyone— and I'm the battery she'll use to level up, Grady thought miserably.

If they told the truth about shooting Daw, then at least we won't be apart for long.

That thought nearly made his heart stop, and the ache punched the breath from his lungs. *No, they had to be lying. I don't want to believe he's gone. I won't. Since I'm not going to get the chance to find out, I choose to believe he's alive. He has Denny and Colt and Knox to take care of him if he got hurt. He'll be a mess with me gone, but they'll keep him from being alone.*

At least we found our way back to each other. We had this year together. Friends, again. Partners. Lovers. Not a bad last year on earth, but I want so much more time together.

I want us to get old and quit hunting and spend our days fishing and reading. Going for walks in the woods without chasing something or being chased.

All those honeymoon plans...vacations. Long weekends. Lazy days where we'd never get out of bed. I thought we had time.

I know he loves me, knows how much I love him. I wish we'd had the chance to get married.

Doesn't look like I'm going to have long for regrets.

Grady needed to bide his time until the others weren't watching him closely. He focused on his memories of Dawson, from long ago, and then this last, wonderful year together. He skipped the times they'd been at odds and only relived the best moments.

I don't want to leave Daw. So I've got to fight to survive—and get back to him.

Footsteps roused him from his memories. He didn't open his eyes, although he knew it had to be Ophelia.

"Pretend to sleep if you want. I don't care. I'll save most of your energy for tomorrow, but you're so luscious, I can't resist. I need to have a taste."

She came closer, and Grady tensed, expecting a blow. He wondered if he could knock her down and strangle her with his chain.

"You can't overpower me. Don't try," she warned. "I'd hate to damage you before the ritual, but my men can beat you senseless without killing you."

Grady considered making an attempt, even if he was doomed to fail. *If I get the shit beat out of me, I can't make a break for it tonight. I'll take whatever she does to me to have a chance to get away.*

Ophelia moved closer, backing him against the wall. She knelt in front of him and straddled his knees.

Grady kept his eyes shut and turned his face away. He didn't know what taking his energy involved, but he knew that anything Ophelia did would be a violation.

Ophelia cupped his face in her cold hands. Grady braced for pain, expecting to be forced to open his mind to Ophelia.

Instead, he felt icy tendrils slide into his thoughts from every direction, black tentacles that wormed into his brain despite how he tried to close himself off to her power.

Trapped again by her spell, Grady couldn't move or speak. He knew Ophelia enjoyed his helplessness, reveled in having the son of her enemy completely at her mercy.

He felt the energy drain like giving blood, a sudden chill in his veins. Ophelia moaned, and Grady wondered if there was a sexual component to her magic.

One of the goons cleared his throat loudly. "Ma'am. Remember tomorrow."

With a snarl, Ophelia pulled her hands away abruptly, ripping her magic from Grady's mind. He gasped. Every tendril of her power felt like it left a bloody trail behind.

Ophelia crawled off him, and Grady fell forward. His chains clanked against the floor. The paralysis spell eased, but he had no will to move.

What will it feel like when she drains everything from me? Will I go cold and tired, like bleeding out?

There are worse ways to die. Burning, like my grandparents and Daw's parents. Bitten by a werewolf and then shot, like Dad. Maybe I'll go to sleep and not wake up. Not a bad death, considering the options. And no blood— easier on Daw when he finds my body.

I've got to get my shit together. I need to pick the locks and run away. I can't let her win this easily.

A faint song filled his thoughts, sweet and distant. The familiar strain wrapped around Grady, soothing the mental wounds of the witch's power. It brought comfort and a sliver of hope.

The mountains are singing me home.

Grady woke just before sunset. He remained still, listening. No voices came from the kitchen, only muted snoring from what he guessed was the couch in the living room. After a few moments, Grady began to move slowly, trying to avoid the clink and drag of his chain against the floor as he strained to reach his wallet, wriggling it loose from his back pocket.

He worked the hidden lock pick against the tumblers in his cuffs. It took concentration due to the odd angle required to use the tool, but finally the cuffs dropped into his lap with just the slightest jangle.

Grady pulled a long, thin, iron nail from the spine of his wallet and put his billfold back in his pocket. This was a weapon of last resort, which pretty much described his situation.

He rose to his feet, wary and hyper-alert, expecting to be caught at any moment. Grady maneuvered around the sleeping man on the couch, surprised and relieved to find no other sentry between him and the door.

Outside, the cool air smelled of moss and ozone. Grady froze and listened, wondering if Ophelia had hired muscle patrolling the territory. When he heard nothing amiss, Grady moved swiftly and silently, trying to put as much distance between himself and the cabin as he could.

The woods were quiet, but Grady couldn't shake the feeling of being watched. He quickened his pace, worried that he might be stopped by a magical barrier that would sound an alarm.

Where the break in the tree canopy revealed the sky, Grady navigated by the position of the setting sun. In the growing darkness, he listened to the songs of the mountains as his guide.

"Grady—I know you're out there," a man's voice called. Daelin's honeyed tones were as beguiling as his glamoured beauty and just as false, Grady suspected. An inhuman shriek broke through the illusion for a few seconds at a time, reminding him of Daelin's true form.

Grady ran faster, focused only on getting away. He felt the toll of Ophelia's energy drain, not fully restored by uneasy rest, and wondered how long he could run. *Can a human outrun a fae?* He doubted it since his pursuer was immortal.

If I can't get away, can I cheat Ophelia of her victory and buy time for Denny and the others to find a way to stop her? Grady recalled the ledges that claimed the two hikers and that nearly added him to the body count.

She can't drain my energy if I'm already dead.

He recoiled from the idea as soon as it formed, knowing that if Dawson was still alive, he would never recover from such a loss. *I want to live. I want to escape. But if the only way to stop her from opening the mound and unleashing the dark fae is for me to die first, then what I want doesn't compare to saving the world—and the people I love.*

"Oh, Grady," Daelin called, taunting him like this was a sick, fucked-up game of hide-and-seek. "Come out, come out. The party hasn't begun yet."

Grady thought he saw the silhouette of a slim man dressed all in gray to his left, and then up ahead, before he vanished and appeared on his right.

Fae move between our realm and theirs. How do I outrun that?

He resolved to keep running until he dropped in his tracks or dove from a ledge if it was impossible to get away. The cool air burned in his lungs, and he gave up on stealth, crashing through the underbrush in a desperate bid for escape.

A row of white mushrooms gleaming in the moonlight brought him up short. Grady looked from one side to the other and realized from the curve of the line that he was in even more trouble than he thought.

Holy shit. I'm on the inside of a huge faerie ring. The whole damn cabin is inside the ring—and probably the mound too.

Grady ran for the boundary, only to be brought up short just as his boots were about to cross when a glowing white lash snapped out to circle his wrist and yank him back.

Daelin appeared to his right with a smile that exposed a mouthful of pointed, shark-like teeth. With horror, Grady realized that the whip looked like a human spine.

"You're not going anywhere," Daelin assured him, yanking on the lash so that it cut into Grady's wrist, burning cold like frostbite.

"But in case anyone is foolish enough to venture out looking for you, I'll make sure they have a merry chase," the dark fae added.

Daelin muttered a few words, and a ghostly figure appeared beside him. Grady gasped as he realized the image was an exact duplicate of himself.

"Like my creation?" Daelin asked. "It's a fetch. Your spectral double. And, oh yes—a death omen. But you know your fate already."

Daelin waved his hand, and Grady's doppelgänger walked off, easily crossing the mushroom circle, to disappear into the shadows. His heart sank, knowing that anyone searching for him would take that apparition to be his ghost.

"Fuck you!" Grady threw himself toward the mushroom line, but the bone-white leash held firm, jerking him back hard enough that he sprawled, face-down on the loamy ground, blood dripping from his wrist where the vertebrae whip had cut into his skin.

He had one small gambit left, more an act of defiance than anything he truly thought might win his release. But Grady resolved not to go down without a fight. He lay still, waiting for Daelin to approach, with the iron nail gripped in his free hand like a dagger.

"Get up," Daelin ordered. "I've had enough of your nonsense."

Grady shot to his feet with the nail clutched in his fist and slammed it into Daelin's throat.

Blinding white light made Grady twist away, and a banshee-like scream threatened to pierce his eardrums. He tried to jerk free of the bone whip while pain distracted his captor, only to be cruelly disappointed when the lash remained tight.

"You worthless wretch!" the dark fae screeched as the light faded. To Grady's horror, Daelin's throat bore only a faint shadow of a wound which vanished as he stared.

"When the time comes, I will cleave open your ribs and rip out your heart as tribute with my own hands," Daelin threatened.

Between one breath and the next, the bone whip uncoiled from Grady's wrist and wrapped itself around his throat, nearly cutting off his air, burning his skin like dry ice.

Daelin turned his back and jerked the whip like a leash, forcing Grady to stumble after him to keep up on the hike back to the cabin. Any time Grady lagged, the bony lash tightened on his windpipe, making him wheeze for breath, digging into his flesh.

The dark fae stormed into the cabin, slamming open the door with a wave of his hand. When Ophelia's two guards appeared from the shadows with guns raised, another gesture from Daelin sent them flying across the room.

Ophelia stalked forward to challenge him, eyes wild with rage. "What is the meaning of this?"

Daelin yanked Grady forward and forced him to his knees before finally releasing him from the bone whip. Grady heaved for breath but vowed that he would not give either Daelin or Ophelia the satisfaction of seeing his fear or his dashed hopes of escape.

"He got out. You need to be more careful," Daelin snapped as if Ophelia were an errant pupil. "Can't work the ritual without him. You need the blood of a King to break the old covenant."

Grady didn't think he could feel more fear, but a new frisson slithered down his spine. *The blood of a King. I'm a King by name but not by blood. Maybe Richardson blood will be what saves us all if sacrificing me fucks up the spell.*

I've screwed up escaping, and I can't fight my way free. But maybe, just maybe, I can still turn the tables somehow. For Daw. For family.

9

DAWSON

"Grady's gone," Dawson said when Denny picked up his call. "He was right behind me, and there was an SUV, and then Gray vanished—"

"Slow down, boy. You aren't making a lick of sense. Start over and tell me what happened."

"Gray was right behind me leaving the shop. We crossed the street, and a white SUV pulled between us. Then Gray was gone. Someone must have snatched him and dragged him into the car," Dawson said, fighting to stay calm and knowing he was losing the battle.

"I've been driving around for a half hour, trying to catch a glimpse of them, but they've just...disappeared," he said, admitting defeat. Dawson had pulled into a parking lot, not sure that he trusted himself to talk and drive with how rattled he felt.

"No one disappears into thin air with a whole SUV," Denny told him. "Call your fed friends and come to the house. I'll have food. In the meantime, tell me the intersection where they grabbed him, and I'll see what I can get from the traffic cams."

Dawson repeated the information and promised Denny he'd be

there soon. He thumbed Gibson's contact on speed dial, gratified when the TBSI agent picked up his call.

"Grady's been kidnapped—and I think it was Ophelia," Dawson said and repeated what he had told Denny. "I'm going after him. I'd appreciate backup, but I'm going one way or another."

"Slow down," Gibson replied, and Dawson heard a muffled recap as he relayed comments to Tucker. "Don't do anything stupid—or at least, don't do it without us."

"I'm heading to Denny's. Can you meet me there? We can plan our attack. I've got some ideas."

"Ophelia's not at her full strength, but she's still a powerful witch," Gibson cautioned. "We need to be strategic."

"She kidnapped Grady!"

"And the only way we might get him back alive is by not running in blindly," Gibson snapped. "We can meet you at your uncle's house in twenty minutes. Go there and stay there—we'll be right along. Got some additional tidbits to share as well."

Dawson ended the call and dropped the phone onto the seat. "Fuck!" he shouted to the windshield, slamming his palms down on the steering wheel in pure frustration.

Desperate, he dialed Sheriff Rollins. "What is it, King? I'm up to my ass in alligators."

"Grady's been kidnapped. We think it's the same witch who killed my parents and Grady's grandparents."

"Goddammit, King! Why is it always something?" Rollins growled. "I've got one of my deputies cooling his heels inside a cell alongside that asshole who tried to burn down the hardware store because he was going to let him escape. Caught them red-handed. Some damn Supernatural Protection Society shit."

"The witch—"

"Then a warehouse blew up on the edge of town—got a tip it was those HDF bastards, but they blew their own asses sky high along with the building," Rollins said. "Now you've got a witch out for your hide?"

"She's behind the Bushwhacker murders," Dawson told him. "Those dead coyote shifters? And the HDF bikers? We think she's backing both sides and siccing them on each other."

Dawson could practically imagine the frustration on the sheriff's face, but Rollins hadn't hung up on him, so at least the man was listening.

"Those Bushwhacker deaths are out of my jurisdiction," Rollins said. "And you didn't hear it from me, but I wouldn't trust the sheriff up there as far as I could throw him. Pretty damn sure he's HDF himself."

"Look—I know you're stretched thin. But if your patrols happen to go by our houses or shops, please keep an extra eye out. I'm afraid someone will try arson again."

"I can't promise anything."

"I know, but...if you've got someone in the neighborhood, I'd be grateful," Dawson said.

Rollins sniffed. "A King, grateful? Where will you be that you can't watch over those places yourself?"

"Rescuing Grady. Stopping a witch. Solving the murders of my parents and Grady's grandparents—maybe Uncle Aaron too."

"You really believe that?" Rollins's voice made Dawson sure the sheriff was scowling.

"Yes. I do."

"You know I didn't like your dad or Grady's dad—but I didn't want them dead. If those weren't accidents, and you can get justice, I'll be glad for you—and lend a hand if I can."

Dawson was silent, floored by Rollins's comments. "Thanks."

"Dawson—" The sheriff never used his given name, so that made him pay attention. "We haven't found any of the Bushwhacker kidnap victims alive. I hope Grady's the exception." Rollins sounded sincere.

Dawson fought the rock in the pit of his stomach at Rollins's warning. "I have to believe I can save him," he managed, as his throat constricted and he held back his feelings. "There really isn't any other option."

Rollins's words kept repeating in Dawson's mind as he drove. *Never found a kidnap victim alive.* He struggled against the grief that threatened to well up in him, the fear that said he'd never get to propose to Grady.

I won't give up until I know for certain. Until I see him...I won't give up. Dawson stuffed his feelings down, resolute. *There'll be time enough to grieve if I fail. But right now, I need a clear head. Grady's depending on me.*

The dark skies mirrored Dawson's mood. Gusts of wind sent leaves and debris flying, bending the trees and making the street signs shudder.

Hell of a day for a rescue. Looks like a bloody fuckin' hurricane's on the way.

He reached Denny's place ahead of Gibson and Tucker. Angel came out to the porch to greet him, wagging her whole back end. Dawson pulled out a half-eaten bag of pretzels from his jacket pocket and shook the last few into his palm to give the Rottweiler, who rewarded him with a slurp of her long, rough tongue before padding away to enjoy her treat.

Denny let the screen door slam, attracting Dawson's attention. "Feeding Angel again? She's not going to be much of a watchdog if she can't fit through the door."

"She barks her head off at squirrels. Maybe we should rethink the true danger." Dawson's snark hid his panic. Denny knew him well enough to understand.

"Bewitched or possessed squirrels would be a hell of a problem," Denny agreed, tongue-in-cheek. "Come inside. Dinner's almost ready. I even made enough for your fed friends." He turned back toward the house before mumbling, "never thought I'd see the day."

Dawson hung his jacket on a peg inside the doorway and headed for the kitchen, just a step behind Denny.

"How are Colt and Knox?"

Denny snorted. "Well they were fine until your call. Now Knox wants to go looking for Grady, and Colt's threatening to tie him to the bed."

"TMI," Dawson protested, unable to resist the humor even now.

"You boys are gonna be the death of me yet," Denny muttered.

The black Corvette pulled up outside, and Angel barked like she would rip the newcomers apart. Dawson glanced at Denny. "You okay having federal agents in the house? Did you hide anything illegal?"

Denny shook his head. "As if I'd leave anything important out in plain view. Not like I'm going to offer them a tour. Just don't take them into the basement. Or the root cellar. The attic's off-limits, and so's the office. Shit—don't let them out of the living room."

"Got it," Dawson replied. "If they need to pee, we've got plenty of bushes."

"Idiot," Denny said fondly, giving Dawson a light slap upside the head.

Colt and Knox came into the kitchen. "Are those the feds?" Colt asked.

"Yep. Play nice. They're here to help," Dawson warned.

Gibson knocked at the door. Angel barked again but silenced at Denny's command and trotted off to sit sullenly in her bed at the end of the room. Denny opened the door, and Gibson peered around the corner.

"Are we going to be dog meat?" he asked, in a tone that suggested he was only partly kidding.

"Not today—if you're good." Denny stepped back to let the two men enter.

"In case anyone here hasn't met, these are Agents Gibson and Tucker. And this is my Uncle Denny, Grady's brother Knox and his partner Colt—and Angel." Dawson said.

"Angel?" Tucker asked with a raised eyebrow and a smirk.

Angel heard her name and wagged, thumping her stubby tail against the cushion.

"Let's eat, and then we can go into the living room and talk," Denny said. "I've got a fresh pot of coffee if anyone wants some. We've got a rescue to plan."

They helped themselves to bowls of homemade chili with all the toppings, along with plenty of chips and salsa, and a pitcher of iced tea. They made short work of eating, eager to get down to business.

Denny brought in an extra chair from the kitchen, and everyone found a seat in the next room. Angel slunk over to sit between Denny's chair and the couch as if she wanted to be involved.

Outside, the wind lashed rain against the windows and howled across the chimney. Dawson wondered if the weather would help or hinder their efforts to find Grady.

Gibson cleared his throat. "The HDF and SPS activity is what initially brought us to the Kingston area. I'm well aware that usually law enforcement cedes coverage of the Cunanoon Mountain area to the Kings, but the domestic terrorist threat was deemed too large for us not to investigate."

"Makes sense," Denny replied with a shrug. "We were aware some crazy folks were out there, but not so many or that they were organized."

"We didn't expect that you would," Tucker said. "That's not what you're focused on. So we stepped in, hoping it wouldn't be as bad as we feared."

"And instead, it's worse," Dawson guessed.

"'Fraid so," Gibson answered. "I mentioned before that we originally thought the Syndicate might be behind the terrorists, but they're not. The head vampire gave us his word, and while I don't usually trust vamps, I think he was telling the truth."

"He admitted that back in the day, he hadn't been happy when Frank and his wife killed the rogue vampire behind the trafficking problem—especially by fire—but he realized that his fledgling had crossed too many lines to defend him," Tucker picked up. "And having human authorities investigate the Syndicate would be much worse."

"That rogue was Ophelia's mentor," Gibson added. "We confirmed that he didn't turn her, but he did teach her magic. The vamp who tried to pick the trafficking back up years later—the one who killed your parents—" he added with a nod toward Dawson, "was her lover. We think Ophelia bound some kind of fire creature to do her bidding when she killed Frank Richardson and Ethan King, but that her control snapped, and she nearly died when it turned on her."

"How powerful is she? What are we up against?" Denny asked.

"Ophelia has a history of stealing magic from other witches," Gibson said. "We think she also gained power from her vampire colleagues, so it weakened her to lose them. After she blew up the plane, we've heard that she was badly injured. If she's doing blood magic to regain power, then the Bushwhacker disappearances are probably a way for her to do that, either by draining the victims of life energy or sacrificing them to a dark entity."

"Fuck," Colt muttered. Dawson stayed silent as fear for Grady knotted in his belly.

"Sacrifice?" Knox repeated, looking like he might go into shock. "*Human* sacrifice? To what god?"

"Not to a god," Tucker replied. "To the dark fae—the fae of the mounds."

"Are you fucking kidding me? How could anyone be that stupid?" Denny exploded. "Rule number one—leave the fae alone!"

Tucker cringed a little at Denny's outburst. "You're not wrong," the agent muttered.

"Back to Ophelia, from what our folks have been able to find out, she's encouraged both the HDF and the SPS—and then played them against each other," Gibson added. "We think she's led them into creating tulpa—thought-form beings—out of their fears to give them something perpetual to fight against. They bring their own worst fears into reality, then have to fight them, reinforcing the fears and making more things to fight."

"Why?" Colt asked, shaking his head in disbelief. "Why would she do that?"

"Distraction," Knox said. "If we're looking at them, we're not looking at her."

Gibson nodded. "Some of that, I think. While Ophelia was

injured, keeping the HDF and the SPS at each other's throats and fighting off their own boogeymen kept any would-be rivals at bay. Now that she's ready to make her big move, she'll let them kill each other without a backward glance."

"She's made a big mistake." Everyone turned to look at Denny. "Adam King, our ancestor who came here from Wales, made a bargain with the fae. We leave them alone, they leave us alone. Blood was spilled, gifts were given. Our family has an *arrangement* with the fae, in perpetuity," he said. "The fae won't look kindly on violating that deal."

Dawson had the feeling that Denny knew a whole lot more about the fae than he let on and decided an in-depth conversation was needed—*after* they stopped the threat and rescued Grady.

"She must think she has a way to open the mound," Gibson said.

"*Opening* the mound isn't the hard part," Denny shot back. "*Controlling* what you've set loose—that's the part that kills everyone in a hundred square mile area. It's the supernatural equivalent of a loose nuke. We've got to stop her. Not just to save Grady—we need to save ourselves and everyone else."

Gibson and Tucker exchanged a glance that spoke volumes. "That man—" Tucker said.

Gibson nodded. "I think you're right."

Tucker turned to the rest of them. "I had a dream where I saw a man in the woods who didn't look like he belonged there. He should have been on some high-fashion runway in Europe. Or maybe be a movie star or a prince. Not someone wandering in the forest. But now —I think he was a fae."

Denny looked up sharply. "The fae agreed to very strict rules about how and where—and when—they could be in our world. Only a few registered representatives are permitted—and only if they technically stay on good behavior."

Tucker snorted. "I guess 'technically' allows for being bankers and attorneys for the legal side of the Syndicate."

Denny ignored the comment. "What the agreement did *not* allow was tampering with human affairs or causing harm. So if we've got a rogue faerie, we're in big trouble—and the fae elders are not going to be happy about it."

"One thing at a time," Dawson argued, feeling like he was going to snap from his worry for Grady. "We need to find Gray."

"We've got the traffic cam footage. We know the SUV that grabbed Grady was headed north," Knox said.

"I had dreams that were just snippets, and I couldn't make sense of them at the time," Dawson confessed. "I saw a white SUV with no license plates—like the one that snatched him. But I also saw a cabin in the woods. At first, I didn't know where it might be. But Gray's got this weird link with the spirits of the mountains."

"When we were out in the woods near where the HDF bikers were found, Gray said that one of the mountains was a bad place and that he felt a strong urge to stay away," Dawson finished. "I'd vote for that being the first place to look."

Denny leaned forward, intrigued. "How does this have anything to do with the spirits of the mountains?"

Dawson turned to his uncle. "Gray can hear them—the genius loci of the hills. I think he's always had it, but before, he never let himself fully believe in it. Lately, he's been listening without prejudice. That 'song' helps him navigate and apparently gives him a nudge now and then, a hunch that turns out right."

A crack of lightning made Dawson flinch. "I'm going after Gray. You can come with me—or not—but I'm going."

"Hell of a storm," Tucker noted. "Not the best for a fight."

"Doesn't matter. Gray's out there, and the longer it takes to find him, the less chance we have of bringing him back," Dawson said. "Tomorrow's the full moon, so if Ophelia's working magic, we're running out of time."

"He's right," Denny said. "There's something cockeyed with the fae angle. I don't know yet what it is, but if it comes down to it, y'all handle the witch, and I'll deal with the faeries."

"We're in," Gibson said with a quick glance at Tucker, who nodded.

"So are we," Colt and Knox spoke at once.

Denny shook his head. "You two need to hold the fort." He raised a hand to forestall argument. "If Ophelia is the one pulling the strings on the HDF and SPS, she's likely to find a way to send them after us as a distraction. We need someone here to keep an eye on the security cams on the shop and the store and the other house."

"You were in the hospital just a few days ago," Dawson said, looking at Knox. "I know you're feeling better. And I know that it's Grady and you want to help. But you're not one hundred percent yet. We can't protect you in a fight and save him."

Knox glared at him, and Dawson remembered their long-ago staring battles as kids. Finally, Knox dropped his gaze.

"You'd better bring him back alive."

"I will," Dawson promised. *Or die trying.*

"Then let's get going," Denny said. "Time's a' wastin'."

They piled into Denny's truck. It had room for all four, plus Grady on the return trip. Given where they were headed, neither the Mustang nor Gibson's Corvette could handle the mud and poor roads.

Denny drove, with Dawson riding shotgun and the two agents in the back. They'd mobilized quickly once the decision was made. Denny gathered items for spells and dealing with the fae, while the others selected weapons and protections. Denny seemed confident about dealing with the faeries, and Dawson wondered what his uncle knew that he wasn't sharing.

Any other time, Dawson would have asked. Now, his worry for Grady stifled his curiosity.

None of the other kidnap victims have been found alive. Have I already lost him? Is this a "retrieval" instead of a "search and rescue"?

Just the thought that Grady might be dead made Dawson's chest ache, robbing him of breath. *I wasted four years away in the Army. We could have had that time together. I want to have a lifetime together, grow old and retire and go fishing and watch sunsets.*

He choked back tears and focused on shifting grief into fury. *This fucking witch has cost our family everything—Mom and Dad, Uncle Aaron, Frank, and Rebecca. Almost got Knox. I will not let her have Gray.*

And if I'm too late...I will burn her and her accomplices to ash.

"Don't borrow trouble," Denny said quietly, without taking his eyes off the road. "We won't know until we get there."

Dawson nodded silently, staring at the downpour through the windshield. The wind swayed the trees, and lightning split the clouds. Thunder echoed, far too close for comfort.

They had narrowed their targets before leaving Denny's house. Satellite photos revealed only a couple of houses on the mountain that Grady indicated had bad mojo. Not surprising if others had even the slightest sense of the malicious energy.

Two of the properties were located low on the mountain and looked too large, modern, and upscale to be right. The third matched the cabin from Dawson's vision—an old cabin halfway to the peak. It didn't photograph well, and Dawson chalked that up to magic. *We only get one shot. I hope to hell we're right.*

Their rain slickers and boots offered limited protection in the storm. Denny parked a mile from the cabin, and they climbed out of the truck. Tucker and Denny brought duffels full of equipment, and they all carried enough weapons to launch a small war.

A few minutes before midnight. Are we too late?

Wind and rain had turned the ground to mud. A torrent of water poured down a swale beside the dirt road. Dawson wondered what sentries might be guarding the cabin. In the distance, he saw a dim light from the windows.

Hang on, Gray. We're coming.

"This place stinks of blood magic," Gibson murmured, a reminder that the TBSI agent was also a witch.

Dawson caught a glimpse of a gray figure among the trees, and he gasped. When the ghostly image turned toward him, he could see the face clearly. "Grady?" Shock nearly took him to his knees. Dawson's thoughts went blank with grief. *He's dead. We're too late.*

Gibson's hand closed on his shoulder. "That's not Grady. It's not even a ghost. It's a fetch." Gibson made a dismissive gesture, and the apparition vanished. "This is why it's handy to have a necromancer around."

"But fetches are death omens," Dawson said, barely able to breathe. The cold rain numbed his body, but nothing could dull the pain in his heart.

"Or they're sent by someone with power who wanted a distraction," Gibson said grimly. "They're a type of fae. I can see the ghosts that are gathered here. Grady isn't one of them."

Dawson felt dizzy with relief and tried to catch his breath. Denny stopped and flung out an arm to stop the others.

"Step carefully—faerie ring," he growled and pointed to the mushroom circle.

A shot rang out, hitting a tree behind Denny. Dawson and the others ducked and scrambled to avoid presenting clear targets.

"Federal agents! Put down your weapons. We will shoot to kill," Gibson shouted into the darkness.

Another shot fired, and Tucker shot back. The gunman fell from the cabin porch as four others loosed a barrage of bullets. All around them, the wind drove the rain hard enough to sting, lightning streaked across the sky, and thunder boomed far too close. One jagged streak hit a tree in the distance with a resounding crash. The air smelled of ozone and wood smoke.

Dawson heard a bullet whizz by and felt a tug on the material of his jacket, only to realize that the new hole in the fabric indicated a near miss.

"Cover me," Denny told him, falling back into the shadows to prepare the ritual items he'd brought in his pack.

Dawson shifted to return fire and shield his uncle. Gibson and Tucker kept up a steady volley, and the number of shooters dwindled until the night went silent.

"Six souls," Gibson told them. "The guards are all dead."

A deep growl came from the darkness near the cabin. Red eyes gleamed from the shadows, and a misshapen creature emerged, its attention fixed on them. It bared long fangs and slowly advanced. When it came into the dim light from the cabin, Dawson could make out the huge form of a hellhound, bigger than a man, powerfully muscled, lantern-jawed.

Gibson muttered something that sounded like a spell, but the hound kept coming. Tucker opened fire, but nothing slowed the creature.

"*Stedda. Arhosa,*" Denny shouted the words in what Dawson guessed might be Welsh.

Immediately, the creature sat.

"*Dere!*" Denny commanded. "Don't hurt him. I just told him to 'come.'"

"Are you fucking nuts?" Gibson countered, wide-eyed.

Denny gave the agent a stern look. "This is Cunanoon Mountain. That's Welsh for 'hellhound.' The *cwn annwn* are protectors of the Kings in these hills, by order of the fae elders."

The huge creature padded over to stand in front of Denny. "*Bachgen da,*" he said. "Such a good boy," he repeated in English.

A shriek of frustration sounded from the vicinity of the cabin. In response, shadows twisted and writhed from beneath the porch, smelling of sulfur and grave rot.

"What the fuck are those?" Tucker yelped.

"The Sluagh," Denny said.

"Spirits of the unforgiven dead," Gibson answered at the same moment. "Probably the real Bushwhacker gang and their accomplices."

Green ghosts took shape, dozens of them, horribly illuminated by flashes of lightning. They looked like half-rotted corpses, still wearing the tattered remnants of the clothes they died in, hollow-eyed. Violent lives and deaths brought them no peace as restless spirits. Malice contorted their faces as they surged toward Dawson and the others.

"Stop now!" Gibson ordered, one hand raised, palm out, toward the specters. The tone of command in his voice brooked no defiance, and the revenant horde froze.

"*Ymosod!*" the panicked voice from the cabin's porch shrilled. Dawson didn't need to understand the words to know the spirits had been told to attack.

"Not going to fucking happen," Gibson shouted.

He looked to the damned souls with compassion. "Go in peace. He has no authority over you. Be at rest." Gibson closed his eyes, and his expression shifted to deep concentration. The green ghosts vanished as if they had melted away with the storm.

Behind them, in the shadows, Denny mixed items in a silver chalice and began to chant an invocation.

"How dare you!" Two figures stood on the porch. One was a slim, elegant man who fit Tucker's vision. The other was a very ordinary looking woman, and Dawson realized with a shock that she had to be Ophelia Locklear, the witch who had caused so much harm.

"I am Daelin, a prince among the fae. My witch and I will destroy you, and then we will scour this mountain," he shouted.

A wave of power swept toward them, bending the tall grass in its way—and meeting an immovable barrier in Gibson's magic.

"Hurry up," Gibson said through gritted teeth. "I can't hold him off long."

Denny shouted the triumphant end to his invocation in a language Dawson didn't recognize. A white dot of light, bright as a star, opened to become a jagged tear in mid-air in the center of the faerie circle.

"No! No! You can't!" Daelin screamed, staring at the light in terror.

The hellhound snarled and bounded toward Daelin, pinning him under his massive paws, fanged maw hovering over the man's throat. The blast of power cut off abruptly.

A shadowy figure appeared from the cabin doorway, and while Ophelia's attention was on the hellhound, he swung a machete and took her head clean off.

The white light faded, leaving an older man dressed in an immaculate white bespoke suit of exquisite tailoring. A piercing whistle drew the hellhound from its prey, and it came to the stranger's side like a well-trained guard dog.

"Daelin. You have gone much too far," the man said in a grave voice, ignoring everyone else.

Daelin tried to scramble away. "Anyon—don't do this. It's not what you think—"

"I *think* you have broken a very old agreement. You have *compromised* the honor of our people. And you intended to do much worse by freeing the fae of the mounds," Anyon snapped, with a thunderous expression. "You are renounced. Your powers are cut off. And you will return with me to meet your judgment."

Anyon clapped his hands, and both Daelin and the hellhound vanished.

Denny moved up beside Gibson. "Honored Elder. Welcome." He repeated the greeting in Welsh and made a formal bow.

Anyon turned, acknowledging them for the first time with a slight incline of his head. "Dennis King. Keeper of the Book. It has been a very long time since your family has called upon me. You have done me and our kind a great service by bringing the traitor to my attention. You have our gratitude."

"The agreement holds?" Denny asked, standing tall—respectful but not subservient to the immensely powerful being in their midst.

A slight smile twitched at the corners of Anyon's mouth. "The Accords are unbroken. Our agreement holds." He looked from Denny to Dawson. "I see the fire in the King blood has not diminished. Watch over these mountains with the blessing of my people."

The white light flared brightly enough that Dawson threw an arm up to shield his eyes. When his vision cleared, Anyon and the light were gone.

"Grady," Dawson breathed, heading for the cabin at a run, ignoring the voices that urged him to be careful.

He came to a dead stop at the foot of the cabin's stairs. Grady stood hidden in the shadows, blood soaked, wrists chained, holding a machete in one hand.

He was the most beautiful thing Dawson had ever seen.

"Daw—are you real?" Grady asked in a shaking voice.

"I'm here, Gray. Real. Denny and Gibson and Tucker are here too. We came to rescue you." He took in Grady's appearance with a deep sense of pride at the sheer stubbornness it had taken his boyfriend to kill his captor. "Looks like you did a good job by yourself."

Grady shook his head, still not moving from the shadows. "Just desperate. Wanted to go down swinging."

Dawson recognized shock in Grady's blown pupils and spacey tone. "Gray—how about you drop the machete? Then let's get those chains gone."

Grady looked down at his hands as if they were someone else's. "Yeah. Good idea."

Dawson gently took the machete from Grady's hands. He didn't recognize the weapon, so he figured that Grady had stolen it from his captors. Asking now wouldn't get an answer, given how out-of-it Grady seemed to be.

This high up the mountain, they didn't have to worry about the police arriving unexpectedly. Gibson and Tucker would still have jurisdiction, so even if the cops came, they wouldn't be arrested, but right now all Dawson wanted was uninterrupted time to take care of Grady.

"Let's go inside," Dawson prompted

Grady recoiled from the cabin like it was a house of horrors. Maybe to him, even in his brief captivity, it was.

"Just long enough to wash off the blood," Dawson coaxed. "Denny'll have words if you get blood on his upholstery."

Grady let himself be led inside. Now that the danger had passed, he seemed to have lost his fighting spirit.

Inside the cabin, Dawson guided Grady to sit in a kitchen chair. The light gave him a better look at Grady's injuries, raw wounds around his wrists and neck that looked like burns and cuts.

"Oh my God. What did they do?"

Grady just shook his head. "Later."

Dawson bit back his questions, knowing there would be a better time. "Let's get those cuffs off you."

"Picked them once—they took my tools." Grady's monotone told Dawson all he needed to know about his lover's state of mind.

"You're safe," Dawson reassured. "Gibson and Denny were badass. Tucker held up his end. I shot things. And the hellhound was cool."

He wet a clean dishrag and daubed gently at Grady's injuries. "Are you hurt anywhere else?"

Grady shook his head. "She took some of my energy, but they wanted me in good shape for the ritual."

Dawson winced at how matter-of-fact Grady sounded about his almost-murder.

"The only 'ritual' you're going to be part of is our wedding," Dawson told him. "No monsters allowed."

Grady smiled, but the wan expression seemed strained. Dawson swore he would help put back the light in his partner's eyes.

Dawson struggled not to curse as he tended Grady's injuries. He cleaned the wounds with water, soap, and whiskey and bound them with strips of a clean T-shirt until he could give better care at home.

"He had a whip that was a human spine," Grady said like he was recounting something that happened to someone else. "Said he was the Dullahan, the fae reaper—caught me when I tried to escape."

"You are a badass." Dawson pushed a glass of water into Grady's hand. He suspected that his captors hadn't worried much about giving him food and drink. Grady looked glazed as he accepted the glass and drank it on autopilot.

"You killed Ophelia," Dawson went on, needing to keep talking so he didn't explode or break down in tears. "You got loose and made a break for it against a fae and a witch. You never stopped fighting. Badass."

"I didn't think I'd make it back," Grady said quietly.

Dawson cupped his chin and met his gaze. "I knew we'd find each other. Although you scared the living shit out of me."

Denny came to the kitchen door. "You done? We need to get a move on."

Grady nodded, and Dawson steadied him as he stood. "Yeah, we're ready," Dawson said, trying not to be obvious about hovering behind Grady as they made their way back to Denny's truck.

"We wrecked the fairy ring," Denny said. "And the feds are rigging the cabin to blow as soon as we're gone. That'll take care of the bodies and send a message."

They came to a complete stop when they walked onto the porch. Gibson stood near Ophelia's body, looking down at her kneeling ghost with a thunderous expression.

Is it weird that I'm more surprised that her ghost has a head attached than that he's interrogating a spirit? Dawson wondered.

"Glad you're here," Gibson greeted them without shifting his gaze from Ophelia. "Want you to hear what she has to say." He seemed even more intimidating as a necromancer than as a federal agent.

"How many more of your goons are still breathing?" Gibson demanded.

"They're all dead," the ghost replied, anger lacing her voice. "All the ones who were insiders. The others are hangers-on. Happy?"

"Not yet." Gibson's tone made it clear he was in no mood for Ophelia's attitude. "What else did you put in motion against the Kings?" He closed his fist, and the ghost shuddered. "Tell the truth, or this gets messy fast."

Ophelia's ghost thrummed with malice and rage. "I intended to kill Grady myself. How sweet to use King blood to open the mound. We'd have come for the rest of them afterward. But you ruined it all!" she snarled.

"Are there curses or hexes laid for them? Don't lie to me—I'll know."

"A hex bag at the hospital, nothing else. Daelin promised me the dark fae would finish the Kings for me." Ophelia's fury seemed to drain away at the betrayal and defeat.

"It's time for you to go. May you find in the next realm exactly what you deserve." Gibson closed his eyes and released the tension in his clenched fist, splaying the fingers wide. A crimson rip appeared in the air, stinking of smoke and old blood. Far away screams echoed, and Ophelia's ghost lifted her head, all defiance gone.

"Please, no—"

"I just open the door, lady. I don't pick the destination."

As Grady and Dawson watched, Ophelia's ghost peeled away bit by bit, spiraling off into the red split in the air until the last of her vanished with a piercing, terrified scream.

Gibson bowed his head for a moment, murmuring something Dawson didn't catch. When he raised his head, the powerful necromancer was gone, and he was back to being a federal agent.

"We should go," he said as if what they had witnessed was commonplace.

Maybe for him it is.

Tucker was waiting in the back seat when they got to the truck, and if Dawson caught a whiff of gasoline, he didn't mention it.

"How about if you ride shotgun?" Dawson said to Gibson, knowing that Grady would do better if they sat together in the back since the front had bucket seats.

"Sure," Gibson replied, picking up on the real request immediately.

I owe him. Both of them. They've saved our asses a couple of times over.

Gibson climbed into the front. Dawson helped Grady into the back and waited as he slid across before following. The cabin exploded behind them before they had left the driveway, and Dawson glimpsed flames dancing high against the night sky in the rearview mirror. *At least with the rain, it won't set the whole forest on fire.*

"So the Kings have an 'agreement' with the fae, huh?" Gibson asked as Denny drove.

"Devil's bargain. I suspect you feds know all about those things," Denny replied, keeping his eyes on the road.

"Goes with the territory," Gibson replied. "What's the saying from that British show? 'Needs must when the devil drives'?"

"I never did figure out what that meant," Tucker volunteered, but his grin put the lie to his words

"Kings have been here for a very long time," Denny replied. "And unlike a lot of the English, we respected what the tribes here knew and believed. Protected them as best we could. They knew about the creatures here. We learned from them. They went out of their way to avoid the fae, but where they couldn't, they understood the...complications...of making deals."

"So this 'deal'..." Gibson asked.

"We leave them alone, and they leave us alone," Denny said. "A few fae have permission to spend time in our world, but there is a lot of fine print. The fae are notoriously legalistic," Denny added with a grin. "They like footnotes."

"When did you learn Welsh?" Dawson piped up from the back seat.

"I speak Gaelic too," Denny replied. "I never was as good in a fight as Ethan and Aaron. I was a bookworm. I mean, I can handle myself on a hunt, and I know my way around the weapons, but I'd rather figure out the spells and the lore. So my brothers left me to it, for the most part. When our father died, I became the emissary to the fae— in case something like this ever happened," he added.

Dawson pressed up against Grady from shoulder to hip in the back, holding Grady's hand in both of his. He'd managed to get most of the blood off Grady's skin, but Grady's clothing was still soaked and it stank in the close confines of the car. Dawson couldn't care less, not if it meant that his lover was alive and next to him.

"I'm sure Ophelia planned to steal Daelin's magic from him, the way she did from all the other witches," Gibson observed, changing the subject. "It didn't exactly go as she planned. I wouldn't be surprised if Daelin intended to kill Ophelia and her goons or feed them to the mound creatures. They were both the double-crossing type."

"If she was really behind the HDF and the SPS, what happens to them with her gone?" Dawson couldn't help wondering aloud.

"Chaos. Anarchy. They'll claw each other to pieces trying to pick new leaders," Tucker replied. "That's assuming, after what happened tonight and the explosion in town, there are many of them left. We've got what we need to go after them—shut them down and haul them in. Can't promise others won't pick up where they left off, but we can wipe the slate clean for now."

"Thank you," Dawson said, squeezing Grady's hand as he spoke. "You guys really came through for us."

Gibson turned in his seat to flash a cocky grin. "That's what we do. Glad to be of service." His eyes took on a teasing glint. "You're not too shabby yourselves—for civilians."

"I can make you walk," Denny threatened. "Don't test my patience."

Gibson raised his hands in surrender. "Yes, sir. Wouldn't dream of it, sir. Right you are, sir," he joked.

"Fucking feds," Denny muttered, but the grin took the heat from his comment.

EPILOGUE

GRADY

"WE STOPPED HER." GRADY STOOD IN FRONT OF HIS FATHER'S BLACK granite headstone in the King family plot of the cemetery. "Dawson and Denny and some friends and I ended it. She cost us all so much —but it's over now. You can go in peace...all of you."

He looked toward the marker for his grandparents and Dawson's parents, all victims of Ophelia's power. Grady didn't know if any of them had chosen to stay behind as spirits, but if unfinished business bound them here, it was high time they were released.

A light breeze stirred, and he chose to take that as confirmation that his comments had been heard.

Dawson wrapped an arm around his shoulders. "They know," he said quietly. "I'm sure of it. If they hadn't already gone on, I hope they can rest now."

"When I was in the cabin, and I was drained and hurt, the mountains sang to me," Grady said quietly as they walked back to the car arm in arm. "They gave me hope."

"You and Knox both have a touch of the 'Sight,' as Denny would call it. Welcome to the club. Makes it damn hard to win at cards if everyone's a psychic," Dawson joked.

"I don't know if the genius loci understand gratitude, but I'd like to plant a tree or build a little shrine or something," Grady confessed once they were back in the car. "Even if they don't notice, it would make me feel better."

"Pick out whatever you want to do, and I'll help you. People all over the world have built spirit houses in places where they sense a presence," Dawson replied. "I think it's a cool idea."

A week had passed since the rescue on the mountain. The newspaper in the town closest to the cabin reported a "fire of unknown origin" at an abandoned building, speculating about lightning strikes from the wild storm that night.

Gibson's magic had cleansed Grady's wounds, which he deemed to be at risk for infection because they were caused by a fae weapon. He hastened healing but couldn't completely prevent scarring, leaving Grady with a thin, jagged, pink scar at his throat and on one wrist.

Grady felt self-conscious about the scars, even though he sometimes rubbed the one on his wrist without thinking.

"They're beautiful," Dawson said, not for the first time, although Grady still didn't quite believe him. "They mean you're still here with me." He lifted Grady's hand and kissed the raised pink lines. "Never hide them. They're battle scars. Be proud of them. Just like I'm proud of you."

Grady felt his cheeks color and tightened his grip on Dawson's hand. "You saved me. I'm proud of you too."

He had welcomed going back to the utter normalcy of the auto body shop as soon as he had recovered enough to last a full day. Nightmares still woke him, but he hoped those would gradually fade. *Our lives create lots of fodder for bad dreams. Goes with the territory.*

Gibson and Tucker had wrapped up their part of the case and headed back to Tennessee with a promise to help out when needed. Knox made a full recovery, which meant he and Colt went back to their apartment, and Denny got his house to himself again.

Sheriff Rollins had let Denny know that the surviving HDF and SPS members were being brought up on a long list of charges, and he hoped that taking a hard line would remind others that they weren't welcome on Cunanoon Mountain. Coming from the grouchy lawman, that was the next best thing to an olive branch.

Grady realized that he'd been lost in thought when he looked up and couldn't immediately recognize the scenery. "Where are we?" he asked as they wound up a twisty mountain road with beautiful scenery and a steep drop to one side.

"It's a nice day," Dawson said, keeping his eyes on the road. "Thought we could take the long way home."

Grady knew the area well enough to realize this route didn't take them home. He stayed quiet, wondering what was going on.

Near the crest, Dawson pulled off at a scenic overlook. They got out and walked to the stone wall, looking over the mountains that were bathed in the late afternoon sun. Dawson wrapped his arms around Grady from behind, and Grady snuggled back against him.

"It's beautiful," Grady said, taking in the view. "It looks so peaceful. Hard to believe from up here all the crazy that goes on."

"I don't care about the crazy as long as I'm with you," Dawson murmured, nuzzling Grady's ear.

It took Grady a moment to realize what was happening when Dawson slid down to his knees and turned him around to face him. Grady was just about to make a smart remark about scenic blow jobs when he realized Dawson had a small black box in his hand.

"Grady King. You are everything to me. I want us to be together forever. Will you marry me?" Dawson sounded nervous, and the worry in his eyes was at odds with his big smile. He opened the box to reveal two matching rings.

Grady folded his hands around Dawson's and the box and sank to his knees to face him. "Yes. I'll marry you. I never want us to be apart again." He leaned forward and kissed Dawson slow and deep.

When he pulled back, they were both flushed. Dawson took one of the rings and slipped it on the third finger of Grady's right hand. Grady did the same with the other ring, catching his breath as he pushed it onto Dawson's finger.

"A promise—until we get a ceremony scheduled, and we can move it to the other hand," Dawson said. Grady kissed him again.

"I love you," he told Dawson. "I think I've always been in love with you. We've been everything to each other—adding 'husbands' makes it complete."

Dawson pressed his lips to their joined hands. "I love you too. Let's go home and celebrate. I've got some ideas to make it a very *memorable* evening to seal the promise. We deserve a break. Someone else can save the world—at least for tonight."

AFTERWORD

I love to use locations and legends that are real in my books, because it grounds the story in a place and makes it feel more real. The Cragmont Sanatarium existed, although it is long gone. Legends about the fae, "moon people," and the not-deer are part of the stories told in the Western North Carolina mountains. The fae lore goes back centuries or longer to the British Isles.

The Tennessee Bureau of Investigation exists, but I have no confirmation on its supernatural counterpart!

If you've read my other series, you probably picked up on the nods to different characters and situations. The "witch in the Midwest" running a drug ring plays a prominent role in *The Devil You Know* (Witchbane), and the para-tropic pharmaceuticals show up in several books across the different series. Steve and Kyle come from *Flame and Ash* (also the Witchbane series). Seth and Evan, the main characters in the Witchbane series, would also be among the high-powered hackers Denny asked for help, along with Teag Logan (Deadly Curiosities series, written as Gail Z. Martin).

Cory and Max have their own book, *Imaginary Lover*. Max is a King cousin. *Imaginary Lover* is part of the Fox Hollow "neighborhood" of related books, which is also where you'll find the psychics who helped Knox—at the Fox Institute.

ACKNOWLEDGMENTS

Thank you so much to my editor, Jean Rabe, to my husband and writing partner Larry N. Martin for all his behind-the-scenes hard work, and to my wonderful cover artist Natania Barron. Thanks also to the Shadow Alliance and the Worlds of Morgan Brice street teams for their support and encouragement, Ellen and Shirley for Welsh translation, Jason for toxicology information, and my fantastic beta readers: Amy, Carole, Chris, Jason, Kelly, Rosalind, Sandra, Sandy, and Sherrie, plus my promotional crew and the ever-growing legion of ARC readers who help spread the word!

I couldn't do it without you! And of course, thanks and love to my "convention gang" of fellow authors for making road trips and virtual cons fun.

ABOUT THE AUTHOR

Morgan Brice is the romance pen name of bestselling author Gail Z. Martin. Morgan writes urban fantasy male/male paranormal romance, with plenty of action, adventure, and supernatural thrills to go with the happily ever after.

Gail writes epic fantasy and urban fantasy, and together with co-author hubby Larry N. Martin, steampunk and comedic horror, all of which have less romance and more explosions.

On the rare occasions Morgan isn't writing, she's either reading, cooking, or spoiling two very pampered dogs.

Watch for additional new series from Morgan Brice and more books in the Witchbane, Badlands, Treasure Trail, Kings of the Mountain, and Fox Hollow universes coming soon!

Where to find me, and how to stay in touch

Join my Worlds of Morgan Brice Facebook Group and get in on all the behind-the-scenes fun! My free reader group is the first to see cover reveals, learn tidbits about works-in-progress, have fun with exclusive contests and giveaways, find out about in-person get-togethers, and more! It's also where I find my beta readers, ARC readers, and launch team! Come join the party! https://www.Facebook.com/groups/WorldsOfMorganBrice

Find me on the web at https://morganbrice.com. Sign up for my newsletter and never miss a new release! http://eepurl.com/dy_8oL. You can also find me on Twitter: @MorganBriceBook, on Pinterest (for Morgan and Gail): pinterest.com/Gzmartin, on Instagram as MorganBriceAuthor, on YouTube at https://www.youtube.com/c/Gail-

ZMartinAuthor/ on Bookbub https://www.bookbub.com/authors/ morgan-brice and now on TikTok @MorganBriceAuthor

Enjoy two free short stories set in Fox Hollow: Nutty for You - https://claims.prolificworks.com/free/r54nldjv and Romp - https://claims.prolificworks.com/free/I4lCYKli

Check out the ongoing, online convention ConTinual www.facebook.com/groups/ConTinual

Support Indie Authors

When you support independent authors, you help influence what kind of books you'll see more of and what types of stories will be available, because the authors themselves decide which books to write, not a big publishing conglomerate. Independent authors are local creators, supporting their families with the books they produce. Thank you for supporting independent authors and small press fiction!

ALSO BY MORGAN BRICE

Badlands Series

Badlands

Restless Nights, a Badlands Short Story

Lucky Town, a Badlands Novella

The Rising

Cover Me, a Badlands Short Story

Loose Ends

Leap of Faith, a Badlands/Witchbane Novella

Night, a Badlands Short Story

No Surrender

Fox Hollow Zodiac Series

Huntsman

Again

Fox Hollow Universe

Romp, a Fox Hollow Novella

Nutty for You, a Fox Hollow Short Story

Imaginary Lover

Haven

Gruff

Trash and Treasure, a Fox Hollow Novella

Kings of the Mountain Series

Kings of the Mountain

The Christmas Spirit, a Kings of the Mountain Short Story

Sins of the Fathers

Treasure Trail Series

Treasure Trail

Blink

Light My Way Home, a Treasure Trail Novella

Witchbane Series

Witchbane

Burn, a Witchbane Novella

Dark Rivers

Flame and Ash

Unholy

The Devil You Know

The Christmas Crunch, a Witchbane Short Story

Sandwiched, Witchbane Short Story

Made in the USA
Las Vegas, NV
10 September 2022